9 CHRONICLES OF CRIME

R. T. LAWTON

This book is licensed for your personal enjoyment only. Please purchase only authorized editions, and do not participate in nor encourage piracy of copyrighted materials. Thank you for your support of the author's rights.

This is a work of fiction. Names, characters, places, events and incidents are either products of the author's imagination or are used fictitiously. Any resemblance to persons living or dead is purely coincidental.

Copyright © 2019 R. T. Lawton
All rights reserved.

Cover art and formatting services by
Michael Kliewer @ CopterGraphics

CHRONICLES OF CRIME

R.T. Lawton

Table of Contents

THIEVING THE RIDE	1
NOT THAT ONE	11
TO CATCH A SPY	23
ON THE PERFUME RIVER	43
COAL BLACK HEART	64
DEARLY DEPARTED	87
SNITCH	103
SHEPHERD OF THE VALLEY	115
ABSOLUTION	136
ABOUT THE AUTHOR	149
BIBLIOGRAPHY	151
TEASER	153

THIEVING THE RIDE

Lionel Red Shirt sat in the driver's seat where he felt like he had control over whatever might happen here this late autumn evening. A black cowboy hat with beaded hat band tilted down over his forehead far enough to camouflage the deep tan contours of his face, making it hard for any witness to recognize him later in a police lineup.

"Just hold on a few more minutes," he said to his passenger.

Arm's length away on the other side of the pickup, a teenage gang-banger from The Boyz draped himself into the corner between passenger door and the ragged upholstery bench seat. His head of long black hair was encircled with a red bandana, like some actor portraying an Apache warrior in an old Ted Turner Classic. Around his mouth hung a sparse *bandido* mustache, hinting maybe a little Mexican blood had crept into the family's veins when no one was watching. His coat was black, a Raiders NFL jacket same as whites wore on the West Coast. Yet Lionel knew the teenage hood, same as him, was Lakota come up from *The Ridge*, one of eight reservations in the state.

Lionel wondered if the kid had any idea about himself, who he really was or where he'd come from. No matter, a couple more days and it would all be over, the kid gone for good.

They'd been waiting in the long-term parking lot at the Rapid City Airport for an hour now. In the bed of the truck, three battered suitcases huddled plainly visible back near the tailgate. Lionel figured most people walking by in the growing darkness would take the setup as a couple of ranchers flying out somewhere. But the three suitcases were empty, and the trip he and the young hood were planning went straight from the airport parking lot to a secluded garage in the city.

Only now the gang-banger showed signs of impatience.

"I'm gonna have me another beer."

"Don't think so, Bud."

"Hey, the name's Spider."

"That your nickname? You a regular Inktomi, ey?"

"Ink what? You making fun of my tattoos?"

Lionel stared for a minute.

"Your folks never told you the old stories?"

"Grandma told us fairy tales, but I ain't a kid no more."

"Inktomi, the spider, the trickster? Led our people out of the underground and into the sunlight, but then we had to fend for ourselves, couldn't go back to the easy life again."

"Yeah, right."

The gangster reached into a red and white cooler on the floorboards.

"I'm having me another taste, so lighten up."

He popped the top on a beer.

Lionel yanked the can out of the juvenile gangster's

hand and tossed it out the d river's window. The rolling aluminum left a trail of white foam smeared across the black asphalt.

"Don't know what other people let you get by with, but you're working my shift now. No boozing, no dope, no huffing glue."

"I always hold up my end."

"Yeah, well Walter's in charge of this crew. Said he needed one more man for the job. I brought you in. Now your actions get reflected back on me."

That wasn't all Walt had said about picking up a last minute gunman for the job, but Lionel wasn't about to fill the kid in on everything. Some people had to find out the hard way how difficult life could be.

A set of headlights pulled into a space up in the next row of vehicles. Lionel 9pointed a forefinger at the new arrival.

"Relax, kid. You wouldn't have had time for that beer anyway. Your party just showed."

Lionel watched as four young guys wearing straw hats with bright tropical hatbands got out of a white Buick. Laughing and shouting, the group grabbed their suitcases from the trunk and moved off toward the main terminal. One man paused, tipped up a brown bottle, then bent over to set the half–full beer down by the rear tire. He stood and quickly jogged along the row of parked vehicles before catching the rest of his group at the crosswalk.

"See that?" said Lionel. Them hats and suitcases means they're going off someplace warm, maybe one of them Caribbean cruises. Probably be gone a week. That's what we're looking for."

The travelers continued out of the parking lot and disappeared into one of the terminal entrances.

Lionel focused his attention back on his protégé.

"So Spider, you see what the driver did there on his way out? Man tried the handle after he closed the door. Means it's locked."

Lionel gestured toward the vacant Buick.

"So go ahead. Show me your stuff."

The gang-banger glanced at the Buick, then back to Lionel.

"Where you gonna be while I'm doing all the work?"

"I'll be right here in the truck, covering your hind end. Somebody's got to be lookout. You're low man on the totem pole, so it's my choice."

The teenage gangster gave a derisive snort before picking up a black nylon gym bag from between them on the front seat. He opened the passenger door and had one foot out on the asphalt when Lionel stopped him.

"Hold on. Take that damn rag off your head. We're trying to stay low profile here. Keep people from remembering us being in the parking lot."

The kid yanked the red bandana from his head and stuffed the cloth into his jacket pocket before slamming the truck door behind him. Rapidly, he stalked across the asphalt to the driver's door of the Buick. Setting the bag down at his feet, he unzipped the top and drew out a long, flat metal strip which he inserted between the rubber molding and the window glass.

Five minutes later, Lionel watched Spider pull up on the handle and open the door. Removing the slim-jim from the window, the gang-banger got into the Buick's front seat. It appeared to Lionel from where he sat, that his car thieving assistant was rummaging through the console and glove box, then checking above the sun visor. After a while, the young gangster came out of the car and walked back to the pickup. He carried the nylon bag as if not sure what to do with it. The driver's door still hung open on the Buick.

"Now what?" asked Lionel.

"You said find the parking ticket so we could get the car out of the lot. But there's no ticket, you know. The driver must've took it with him. Want me to bust into another car?"

"Give me the damn slim-jim. As long as it took you to crack that lock, we'd be here all night. Some car thief you are."

Lionel grabbed the metal strip.

"I'll find a ticket to get us out. Now go hot-wire that thing. See if you got any talent there."

Checking to ensure no owners were still sitting in their parked vehicles, Lionel moved cautiously through the long-term lot. He tried several cars for unlocked doors, before finding an extended-cab pickup with a parking ticket lying in full view on the dashboard. He pulled on the driver's handle.

Locked.

Sliding the metal strip down the side of the window, Lionel probed for the locking mechanism. With the other hand he tugged on the door handle again.

Two minutes later, Lionel decided this wasn't as easy as it looked and maybe he should try his luck on the other door. Going around to the passenger side, he inserted the slim-jim and tested the door handle for tension. The door swung open.

Lionel grinned.

If it wasn't for fools, this thieving profession wouldn't be so easy.

Looking around again for witnesses, Lionel reached inside, snatched the ticket off the dashboard and closed the door. Hurriedly, he returned to his old pickup, slipped inside and quietly eased the door shut. A quick glance through the windshield told him the youthful gangster was still fiddling under the hood of the Buick. That engine wasn't going to start for a while yet.

Cowboy hat now tipped lower over his eyes with the brim resting on the bridge of his nose, Lionel leaned back in the driver's seat. Listening to the turned down radio, he sipped a beer, waiting.

After a time, Spider finally crawled back into the pickup. Seemed to Lionel like the young gangster had acquired a tone to his voice, almost as if the kid was getting a little cocky about finally getting the Buick to start.

"Find a ticket yet, old man?"

Lionel passed over the manila, time-stamped piece of paper.

Spider took the parking lot ticket without looking at it. "How long'd it take *you* to get in?"

"Two minutes. Easy when you know how."

Spider didn't say anything.

Lionel pushed. "Got our car running?"

The gang-banger nodded.

"Then I'll follow you back to the garage. Just stay out of trouble getting there. I can't baby-sit you forever."

Still wordless, Spider put the ticket in his pocket and returned to the Buick.

After the stolen car backed out of the parking space, Lionel waited a little longer to let its tail lights get a good distance away before he started the old pickup's engine and drove slowly in the same direction. The Buick's brake lights flashed bright down near the exit. Lionel stepped on his own brakes so as not to arrive at the ticket booth too soon. No sense letting the booth attendant relate them together in any way.

The Buick's brake lights stayed on.

Lionel put more pressure on the pickup's brakes.

The Buick showed no signs of leaving.

Having already entered the long single lane from the parking lot to the toll booth, Lionel figured he couldn't back up now without being obvious. The old pickup idled forward as slow as Lionel thought he could safely go. Fifty feet from the toll booth, he reached underneath the front seat and pulled out an orange bath towel. Steering with his left hand, Lionel unwrapped the bundle with his right. He removed a 9mm Sig Sauer and slid it under his right thigh. The automatic was hidden from sight, but close at hand if Lionel thought he needed it. Finally, he pulled up behind the Buick and stopped. The tollgate remained down.

Coming out of the booth, an overweight attendant lumbered back toward the pickup. Lionel lowered his driver's window, wondering what the hell was going on.

"I got my money and my ticket ready," said Lionel, holding up the mentioned items in his left hand. "What's the problem?"

"Your young friend up front doesn't have enough cash, so I can't raise the gate. He says you'll make up the difference for him."

So much for nobody remembering we were here.

"That cheap mother," Lionel muttered in a low voice, but couldn't think of another way out just now. "How much you need?"

"His ticket says the car has been in the lot for two weeks. That comes to forty-eight dollars. Your friend only has ten bucks. You need to come up with thirty-eight more."

Lionel was thinking it was just his luck to steal a parking ticket from a vehicle that'd been here two weeks already. This sort of thing never happened when he worked alone. Some kind of bad karma had to be coming from that juvenile gang-banger, that Spider kid who hadn't made up his mind who he was yet.

Lionel took out his billfold, raked his index finger into a small leather compartment and removed a well-creased twenty-dollar bill folded twice into a small rectangle. He handed it, plus the other twenty already in his hand, out through the window to the attendant who slowly waddled back to the booth.

A few minutes later, Lionel watched the attendant's arm come out of the toll booth window and count off a couple of bills into Spider's outstretched hand. The gate went up and the Buick left.

The gate came down.

Lionel pulled up to the booth. He glared at the attendant.

"You gave my change to that kid. Why in the hell did you do that?"

The attendant gazed complacently back at Lionel.

"Just natural to give the change to the person paying the ticket, I suppose."

"He didn't pay for the ticket, I did."

"That may be, but he's the one who handed me the ticket and it was his car in front of the gate, so I naturally gave him the change when I rang up the register. Now, can I have *your* ticket please?"

Sullenly, Lionel stuck out his hand with the ticket in it.

"That will be two dollars please," said the attendant.

Lionel muttered to himself as he dug through his front jeans pocket for loose change.

First you ding me for forty dollars, now you want two more. If you weren't so dumb, I'd shoot you and drive off.

Lionel handed over six quarters, four dimes, a nickel and his last five pennies, keeping back enough large coins to make a phone call.

The toll gate went up.

"Thank you, sir, and have a good evening."

Headed back to town, Lionel let the Buick's red tail lights disappear in the distance while he stopped off at a pay phone outside a convenience store on East Highway 44. He felt a need to call the telephone number on a slip of paper that Walter had given him earlier. When Walt answered the phone, Lionel made it plain.

"Walter, remember when you told me to get some young, up-and-coming gangster for our little job, but first off he should help me steal our getaway ride?"

"Yeah."

"Said go on up to the Homes in North Rapid and get one of The Boyz? Just be sure when the job was over, that the kid wasn't anyone I would feel bad about later?"

"I remember."

"And then you mentioned that after the job, we'd probably have to draw straws to see who explained to this young gang-banger that he wasn't getting any shares from the heist?"

"Okay. So where you going with all this, Lionel?"

"I just wanted you to know I've already drawn the short straw. Drew it about ten minutes ago. This'll be a permanent discussion between me and the kid. No negotiations, and no comebacks, if you hear what I'm saying."

The silence on the other end of the line grew until Lionel wondered if Walt was still there or had laid the phone down and wandered off for a beer or something. Finally, he heard Walter's voice again, nonchalant and matter of fact.

"Sounds like a personal thing on your part, but okay, you're in the driver's seat for this one if that's the way you want it."

Lionel hung up the phone and adjusted his hat. He was starting to feel back in control again.

NOT THAT ONE

It was on Paddy Kilpatrick's mind that the time had come for him to get out of the business. The word was already out on the snowy streets about his work getting a little sloppy these days. If he wasn't careful, his employers, the Chiavella brothers, could rethink their position on his continued employment. In which case, they just might put out a contract to terminate his contract. "Loose lips sink ships" and "three can keep a secret if two are dead". That sort of stuff.

The situation wouldn't be so bad except the target of his last contract, Lebanese George, had survived the freezing cold in a certain downtown alley on the Kansas side of the Missouri river, not to mention the three 9mm holes in the front of George's chest. And now, Old George was said to be resting comfortably in a nice warm Kansas City, Kansas, Saint Somebody-or-other hospital room. Thus it was settled, Paddy had to make a second effort.

After much contemplation, plus the benefit of the local weather report and various comments of a friend familiar with that particular hospital's procedures, Paddy believed he could take care of two different problems at the same time. But, since both problems concerned his future health, maybe they were related after all. And so he packed the necessary items into a large suitcase, then called for a Yellow Cab early in the evening to drop him off at the Emergency Room entrance. A short distance inside the double-wide doors was the beginning of the hospital bureaucracy.

"That's a rather large suitcase you're dragging behind you," said the elderly Admissions lady after Paddy had explained about his chest pains.

"I'm afraid so," replied Paddy between gasps. "You see, I'm traveling on business, so I had to bring everything with me."

The Admissions lady stared at him.

"Wasn't sure how long I'd be here," continued Paddy in the extended silence, "and there was no place to leave my personal belongings."

"I see, Mister Jackson. Well, just so you don't plan on using our little hospital as a long-stay motel room. We're awfully busy with other patients here you know."

Paddy almost missed the reference to Mister Jackson, until he remembered Jackson was the name on the credit card he was using to fund his physical examination and current hospital program. As it was, he merely needed to ensure his early release from this medical establishment and swift departure from the premises before the card was reported stolen. But then Paddy always took his problems one at a time, as they came.

This old age thing," he told the Admissions lady. "It's getting hard to live with. I mean, I eat Tums by the handful, run out of breath on any kind of stairs and my hair goes AWOL every time I comb it. And that's saying nothing about the cost of dental work these days."

The lady glanced up from the admissions form she was filling out.

"I know what you mean."

Paddy couldn't tell if that was the beginnings of a smile or the makings of a grimace on her face.

She completed his paperwork and called for a male orderly and a nurse.

"Miss Penosa will take you to an examination room where a doctor will see you about those chest pains. And Harry will carry your suitcase. We don't want any heavy lifting on your part just in case you've suffered a mild heart attack."

Within thirty minutes and a few minor medical tests, Paddy had convinced the doctor in the examination cubicle that the safe thing to do was admit him, *Mister Jackson*, to the hospital for overnight observation. Of course, the subtle dropping of the word "malpractice" in juxtaposition with the topic of heart attacks had seemed to clinch the decision. Next thing Paddy knew, Miss Penosa was pushing him in a wheelchair up to a private hospital room on the second floor. Harry, the orderly, was quickly tasked with dragging the overlarge suitcase right behind them.

"Do you want me to help you unpack this?" asked Harry once they were inside the private room.

"Naw, just park it in the closet. I'll get whatever I need later."

Harry stuffed the suitcase into the small upright cubicle and returned to the wheelchair where Paddy remained seated.

"Anything else?"

"Yeah, can you get me a copy of the *Star*? I got money down on the Jayhawks and need to see how they did last night."

"That's easy, KU beat KSU. The Wildcats didn't stand a chance."

"Yes," said Paddy with great enthusiasm. This meant the bookies over on Troost Street were going to owe him a bundle. Of course he'd have to finish this job before he had any hopes of collecting, especially since the Book was another arm of the same organization that employed him to eliminate various obstacles to their many business concerns. He toned down his smile a little.

Harry had remained standing near the wheelchair.

"You still want the paper?"

"Nope. Life is looking good right now and I gotta say you've been a great help," replied Paddy as he tipped the orderly a five dollar bill.

Harry stared at the money as if he wasn't sure what to do with it. Finally, he put the bill in his shirt pocket, nodded once and left the room.

In the meantime, Miss Penosa had laid out a backless hospital gown in a faded blue and white stripe and a pair of soft cloth slippers in the same shade of blue. Now, she stood at the door with an expectant look on her face.

"Hang your clothes in the closet, Mister Jackson, and get right into bed. We'll check on you every hour to make sure you're okay. There's a cord with an emergency push button clipped to the left side of your pillow if you have any more pains. And if you need something to help you sleep just let me know. The doctor will run more tests in the morning."

She closed the door behind her.

Paddy sat in the wheelchair and sniffed the air. Cleaning antiseptics. Seemed like all hospitals smelled alike and he had spent most of his life trying to stay away from that sterile, stringent aroma. Ah well, he should be gone in the next eighteen hours, plus he might get a free physical to boot.

At his age, it never hurt to make sure all his parts were working the way they should. God forbid he should have a case of advanced hidden cancer or a calcifying liver. Best to find these things out early and get them fixed while he could. Especially on someone else's credit card.

Rising from the wheelchair, Paddy tip-toed to the door and opened it a crack. He knew his own room number and by squinting just right, without any eye glasses on, he could barely see the number across the hall. His room seemed to be in the correct neighborhood for what he had in mind. Slightly widening the opening, he observed the young uniform cop sitting in a brown folding chair and reading a sports magazine outside the next door up the corridor. He'd noticed the cop earlier during the wheelchair ride.

"There we go," breathed Paddy to himself. "Now all I have to do is wait for the nice policeman to wander off for a cup of coffee or something. Then me and Lebanese George can have one last visit."

He gently closed the door, undressed and hung his clothes on hangars in the closet. The cloth slippers would work out fine for sneaking quietly from one room to the next, but he wasn't too sure about the hospital gown with the two flimsy cloth ties in the back to keep it closed. The darn thing was drafty when you walked and cold when you sat on vinyl or metal surfaces. No wonder there were so many sick people in hospitals.

Glancing at his watch, Paddy decided to start a mental log to help figure out how much time he'd have to conclude his unfinished business. But first, he had one more task to perform in order to be ready when the opportunity arose. Going to the closet, he dragged the large suitcase out into the room and undid the locks. The exertion glazed his forehead with a light sweat. His pulse increased. Man, he didn't remember the thing being this heavy, but he also knew why it was.

With tired hands – it had been a long two stressful days since the shooting - Paddy opened the suitcase and put on a pair of thin leather gloves. Lastly, he removed a long metal cylinder. This particular metal bottle was painted green to signify that it contained oxygen. Only Paddy knew that under the green paint - paint he'd sprayed onto the metal bottle earlier that morning - was a different color. This now hidden color designated a gas that while not poisonous in and of itself, was very fatal if it gradually replaced the oxygen in a person's blood system.

And, since Lebanese George was sucking up oxygen to keep his lungs going, Paddy's plan was to place the newly painted green bottle next to George's bed so that when his current oxygen bottle ran out, the nurse would naturally hook up the breathing line to the next available green bottle. The scheme was K-I-S-S simple because the hospital was using oxygen bottles while its plumbed-in-the-wall oxygen system was down for repairs. And, with the approaching blizzard blocking the normal supply routes from the hospital's medical supply company, this hospital would have to use whatever medical supplies it had on hand until the snowplows opened the streets again. But the best part of the plan was the difficulty of anyone being able to place the blame on Paddy himself.

Unfortunately, the blizzard could also hamper his strategic withdrawal back across the inter-city viaduct, since that street would then consist of a long ribbon of ice from one bank of the river to the other. Therefore, getting safely back into Greater K C on the Missouri side would become a logistics nightmare. Ah well, one problem at a time.

He stood the green cylinder in a front corner of the closet where it would be handy when he needed it, yet concealed from any unwary nurse that might pop in on him at regular intervals to check his heart rate. At the sound of footsteps now stopping outside his door, Paddy scurried across the room and jumped into bed.

The door opened. Nurse Penosa again.

At the last moment, Paddy remembered to remove his leather gloves and hide them under the sheets. Gloves. One more thing to keep track of.

"Still awake are we?" Nurse Penosa removed Paddy's right arm from beneath the sheet, turned his hand almost palm up and placed her warm fingers along his wrist.

"Guess I'm just a little worried about my condition," he replied.

"Just relax, Mister Jackson. We take good care of all our patients." After a long count, she replaced his arm back under the sheet and pulled the blanket up to his neck. "This is a good night to stay warm, what with the storm outside and all."

"How's my pulse?"

"A little higher than it should be, but with rest you'll do fine."

"Will you be the one checking on me all night?"

"No, I go off duty here shortly. The late night nurse will look in on you from time to time."

"You mean the graveyard shift."

Nurse Penosa paused in the doorway. "We prefer not to use that term here. Our wing looks after some of the more critical cases in the hospital, and that phrase has such a negative connotation. So if you please."

"Right you are," said Paddy. "I won't slip up again. Good night."

She turned out the lights and closed the door halfway. Paddy listened to her footsteps recede down the corridor. Now he was left with the silence of a hospital at night: muted announcements from the paging intercom, squeaky wheels on a passing gurney, the murmur of voices at the head nurse's station. All that and the outside hiss of blowing snow from the expected storm. The plan would work if he were careful.

He hopped out of bed with his slippers still on and hurried across the room. Closing the door to within a few inches for concealment, Paddy peeked down the hall and found a different policeman now on guard outside Lebanese George's door. The replacement cop had white hair and a wide mouthed yawn. Better yet. Paddy glanced at his watch and proceeded to keep note on the policeman's movements. The elderly cop's apparent love for fresh coffee to help keep him awake during his shift also necessitated frequent trips down the hall and out of sight for several minutes. Paddy's chance for closure should come soon.

The only other obstacle to coordinate was the night nurse. Three times, Paddy had heard approaching footsteps and had to race for the bed. Twice, those footsteps had been the night nurse en route to check his pulse. The third set had been a false alarm, but all this sprinting back and forth was starting to wear on Paddy's nerves, to say nothing about the cold breeze flapping on his back. Couple the sweat emanating from these quick dashes along with the open back door of the hospital gown, and Paddy now felt icy fingers running up and down his spine.

On his next trip to the door, at a slower pace this go around, Paddy watched as the old cop stood up from his chair in the hall and hurried off in the opposite direction.

"This is it," Paddy muttered to himself. He raced to the closet and reached for the green metal bottle.

No, no. He needed the gloves. No fingerprints that way.

He ran to the bed and yanked back the sheets. The gloves were here someplace. Quickly he snatched up the thin black leather and pulled one glove over each hand.

Good.

Now he hustled back to the closet and grabbed the metal canister. Man this thing was heavy. Must be about fifty pounds, but felt like more.

Paddy hastened to the door for one more peek.

The coast was clear.

He sprinted across the hall, up a door and into Lebanese George's room. The night light showed a row of three green metal cylinders standing upright on the floor. A breathing tube snaked up from one of the bottles to a clear plastic mask over a man's face as he lay sleeping in the bed. Yep, it was Lebanese George all right, ragged breathing and all. Obviously he was still alive and a bane on Paddy's continued existence.

Paddy gratefully lowered his newly painted green metal bottle to the floor. Damn it was heavy. Then straining to pick up the second bottle in line, he repositioned that cylinder to the end of the row and replaced the vacant space with his own green bottle. Now, whenever George ran out of oxygen and the nurse hooked up the next bottle in line, it wouldn't be oxygen that was being absorbed into George's bloodstream. Bye, bye, George.

Pausing to gulp some air into his own lungs, Paddy heard the pounding of his heart beat inside his inner ear. He needed rest, but one look at his watch told him the cop would be returning at any moment. Quickly, he scooted for the door.

A rapid check in both directions and Paddy dashed across the hall and back into his own room at full speed. He closed the door and slid down the wall. Old age and a hard life on the streets was catching up with him. His lungs heaved like air shocks on a bad road. He felt waves of dizziness and nausea. Definitely time to get out of the business.

As he rested on the cold hard linoleum, he heard the footsteps of the policeman returning from his hasty trip down the hall. Several minutes later, while Paddy still gasped for air and waited for his pulse to die down, the frantic cry for a Code Blue came over the paging system out in the corridor.

Paddy leaned over and placed his ear close to the door. The swish of running medical personnel filled the hallway. They appeared to be converging on a room close by. If it was for Lebanese George, then it was quicker action than Paddy could've hoped for.

All this adrenaline bustling around was exciting. Almost like the old days when he'd scored a kill followed by an immediate all-night celebration on the town with a few of his closest friends. Too bad the circle was growing smaller with the passage of years. And, truth be known, he would miss Lebanese George. They'd had some good times in the old days, before George had gone independent and tried to buck the Chiavella brothers.

"Good luck, George, you're gonna need it."

Thinking maybe he ought to open the door a crack and see for sure this time, Paddy reached for the handle, but his left arm suddenly wouldn't cooperate. The whole arm seemed to tingle with a mind of its own. Paddy tried to stand, only his strength had deserted him. Rolling over on his stomach, he crawled toward the bed. A sharp pain shot through his upper chest. A real pain. Uh oh, he should've waited for the results of the doctor's tests before embarking on this caper.

Now if he could just reach the emergency button, some of that medical help might come take care of him. Forget about Old George, doc, he's not going to make it anyway, not if the man had been sucking out of that second bottle in line.

Sweat rolling off his forehead, Paddy pulled with his right arm and pushed with all his toes to creep across the room to his hospital bed. "Wouldn't it be ironic," he thought, "if I died from a heart attack while completing the contract on George? Surely life couldn't be that cruel, even in my line of work." But, he was in a hospital and it was the medical people's job to save lives. So, rolling into a sitting position, he reached up with his right hand and pushed the button on the emergency cord. Help would come soon.

"Oh, damn, the gloves."

Frantically, Paddy worked the gloves off both hands and threw the black leather under the bed just as his door flew open. His lungs pumped with a leaky wheeze.

"Mister Jackson," cried the nurse, "are you all right?" Over her shoulder she shouted for the second Code Blue of the night.

Paddy heard the pounding of feet now rushing for his door. In a matter of seconds, he was lifted onto the bed and the nurse was checking his racing pulse. Someone called for the defibrillator cart.

Paddy felt a second pain race through his chest. Breathing was becoming such a problem.

An intern rushed into the room with a green metal cylinder. It made a heavy thunk as he dropped the oxygen bottle onto the floor by Paddy's bed.

"I was in George's room when the old guy's body

finally gave out on him," said the intern in a breathless hurry. "Couldn't do anything more there, so when I heard this call, I just grabbed the next unused oxygen bottle in line and hurried over here to help."

"What?" registered in Paddy's mind.

"Good for you," said the nurse. "Hook Mister Jackson up to the bottle so he can get some air. He's got trouble breathing."

"Wait a minute," gasped Paddy. "Not that one."

"Now don't you worry, Mister Jackson. We'll take care of everything. Just relax and breathe deeply."

She placed the clear plastic mask over Paddy's face and held it firmly in place.

For his part, Paddy Kilpatrick tried to hold his breath as long as he could.

TO CATCH A SPY

"Step quiet, lads. The *Kaffirs* say Oom Paul and his Dutch burghers have long ears."

Sergeant Major Toft of the Imperial Light Horse cautioned each group of soldiers passing in the night and out through the last trenches in the final defenses of besieged Ladysmith.

"Wouldn't do to let the Boers know we're coming now, would it? Do this right and we'll have their Uncle Paul Krueger out of the Transvaal by Christmas."

On the other side of the opening, Lieutenant Pierce stood across from the Sergeant Major and counted each soot-blackened face as one soldier after another filed past the outer barricade. One hundred men on foot selected from the Imperial Light Horse by General Hunter himself, plus one hundred Natal Carbineers, a few sappers and miners, and three hundred mounted volunteers. Native scouts had already been deployed as guides across the brushy ground toward Gun Hill.

The mounted volunteers quickly divided into two columns, each column moving far out on either flank as a protective screen for the line of march. These horsemen seemed to drift silently away like apparitions, and soon disappeared into the folds of the South African darkness. No jingle came from their harness or military equipment as the soft plod of muffled hooves on dirt gradually died away.

When the last soldiers on foot left the barricade, Lieutenant Pierce fell in with his rear guard. Mentally, he calculated the distance to Gun Hill. Their time of exposure would be limited, but lately the Boer General Piet Joubert seemed to know their every move. For some reason, ambushes on their patrols and troop movements outside the city had become more frequent. ..and more accurate.

At the tail of the column, Lieutenant Pierce listened for sounds in the moonless night. Here, no noise came from bird or animal, it seemed they'd all fled in the previous weeks of bombardment during the siege. For now, only the subdued tramp of English leather boots came to his ear. No clank of rifle, no thunk of loose canteens, and more importantly, no sound of betrayal to the Dutch.

As the march gradually slowed and came to a quiet halt, the Lieutenant estimated that his foot column had now reached the base of Gun Hill where Boer artillery had been positioned during early days of the siege in order to pour shells into the Ladysmith garrison. Especially the big cannon, the one called "Long Tom," which had enough range to throw artillery rounds into the very heart of Ladysmith without fear of counter-fire from the shorter range British batteries.

At the bottom of the slope, Pierce silently established a skirmish line to secure their avenue of withdrawal, and then sent pickets out to each side to guard his raiders' backs during the assault. All in readiness, he took a runner and moved forward to join the main body of troops moving up the incline. Drawing his pistol, he felt as ready as he was ever going to get for something like this.

Waiting grew short; the need for stealth was done.

From twenty yards below the crest of Gun Hill came the Sergeant Major's bellow, "Fix bayonets!"

A rustling ran through the mass of soldiers poised on the slope.

At once, the South African night seemed to grow even more silent with the listening of a thousand ears.

"Cold steel!" rang the Sergeant Major's voice.

With a rush, troopers went over the parapets of Gun Hill and into the Boers' position. Lieutenant Pierce heard bewildered cries in Dutch and the headlong flight of horses out into the dark. In a rush of adrenaline, he found himself suddenly standing on top of the gun parapets looking down into the Boer encampment, witness to action by both sides. The Boers with their shaggy beards and battered slouch hats erupted from around their campfires, with bandoliers slung over their shoulders, running to their horses. The British charged with rifles at the ready and their military pith helmets bobbing forward like popped corn in a hot skillet. In great haste, the Dutch vacated the ground.

A British cordon was quickly set up around the hill as sappers and miners stuffed gun-cotton charges with two inch fuses into Boer cannons. Red explosions burst gun barrels and breeches. Sledgehammers rang on "Long Tom" as the breech lock was detached and carried away as a trophy of the raid. Scattered shots roared out into the darkness along the perimeter of the cordon.

Two squads of Natal Carbineers wheeled a captured howitzer and a Maxim up to Lieutenant Pierce and breathlessly reported.

"Sir, the General said we should take these with us."

Pierce eyed the two weapons. "Move along then. I'll send my runner on ahead to warn our skirmish line of your approach."

As he turned in the direction of Ladysmith and dispatched his runner down the slope, Pierce registered a flash of light from the distant city. He paused to study the valley before him more carefully. A small white light blinked off and on somewhere inside the defenses of Ladysmith. Yet all of the city was supposed to be under blackout conditions at night to keep Boer gunners from sighting in on any lighted targets.

Quick dots and long dashes of white continued to flash.

Morse code?

But not in English.

Either the message had been encrypted to protect sent information from the enemy, ...or it was in Dutch and the Boer General was receiving information from sympathizers hiding inside the city.

Removing his compass from his tunic pocket, Lieutenant Pierce took a reading on the blinking light. The flashes ceased.

"Lieutenant?"

Pierce spun around as he recognized General Hunter's voice.

"I think we will be retiring now. We've done what we came to do. You'll cover our withdrawal."

"Yes, sir." A pause. Then. "May I have a word?"

"Only if it has to do with any problems regarding our withdrawal. Otherwise it will have to wait. I expect to do this in an orderly fashion."

"Yes, sir."

Without a backward glance, Hunter strode down the

hill and was quickly swallowed up into the darkness. He was closely followed by various groups of soldiers as each squad and company completed its part of the mission and joined the withdrawal. At least this time, there were no dead to deal with, and no wounded being supported by their comrades for the long march back. For once, the surprise had been on the Boers.

Lieutenant Pierce descended from the parapets with the last group of foot soldiers from the Imperial Light Horse. Along the way, he quietly called in the pickets until they joined up with the rear guard's skirmish line. Now, with many a backward glance, and a light tickle of unease at the base of his neck, Pierce gave soft orders to his rear guard troops.

To him, it seemed as though they walked forever, almost blind across the grassy plain, following soldiers in front of them and wondering if the dark, unmoving objects off to the sides were simply low slung bushes or a mounted Boer scout waiting in ambush, a scout with loaded Mauser rifle ready to fire. Ears strained, but no snicker of horse or tick-tick of rifle bolt floated in the night air.

The only sounds carrying through the darkness were soft grunts and muffled curses from the Natal Carbineers wheeling the two captured guns across the bumpy earth ahead of them. As the column neared the outer defenses of Ladysmith, Lieutenant Pierce once again heard the soft plod of muffled hooves on dirt close by. Mounted volunteers, who had acted as a protective screen for the column's flanks, returned to ranks like the dusty ghosts they were. Briefly, he wondered how they'd felt waiting out there in the South African bush, not knowing which way the battle was going. Them seeing the rifles of their comrades blazing pockets of red flame up on Gun Hill and there being little the mounted volunteers could do to help in that part of the action.

Back at the barricade where they had departed the outer trenches earlier that evening, Lieutenant Pierce found Sergeant Major Toft taking count as groups of raiders filed by. From the sound of the senior non-commissioned officer's voice, he was a happy man.

"All the lads have returned safe and sound, sir. Not a scratch on 'em. I'd say we stuck it to the Boer this time if you don't mind me saying so, sir, and brought home two of their guns to boot."

"Perhaps we had a piece of luck, Sergeant Major."

Bringing up the tail of the column, Lieutenant Pierce quickened his pace to keep up with the senior NCO. Now that they were safely back in garrison, the memory of the blinking lights from inside Ladysmith returned to mind.

"I've heard a rumor," Pierce began, "that a good Sergeant Major knows everything going on in his army."

"I've heard that same rumor, sir."

"Then let's give it a test."

The Sergeant Major came to an abrupt halt with his spine ramrod straight and his hands clasped behind his back. His voice carried a slight frost as he took a quarter turn toward the Lieutenant.

"What did you have in mind, sir?"

"I know that General Buller's army for the relief of the siege of Ladysmith is pinned down at the Tugela River crossing. And I know that our signalmen have sent heliograph messages to General Buller's scouts up in the hills in order to keep both Commanding Generals aware of each other's circumstances."

"That's true, sir. Plus, both our lot and General Buller's staff have used native bearers to carry dispatches, however not many of them made it successfully through the Boer lines without getting themselves shot. But do go on, sir."

"What I'm wondering, Sergeant Major, is do we also send out messages with signal lanterns or other flashing lights in the middle of the night?"

"Not to my knowledge, sir."

"And if we did send such messages, would they be directed toward Gun Hill?"

"Wrong direction, sir."

"Then we have a problem in the city."

The Sergeant Major dropped his chin an inch.

"How so, sir?"

"When I was standing on the parapets at Gun Hill, I happened to turn toward Ladysmith and saw a light blinking out Morse Code. Since it was not in clear English and was sent in the wrong direction, I must assume the message was in Dutch for the Boers. That suggests we have spies within the city."

The Sergeant major leaned forward slightly, now speaking in a softer guarded voice.

"I believe you're correct in this thought, sir. And our Commanding General Sir George Stewart White also believes we have spies among us who are working for the enemy, but he speaks of it only in private. That's why tonight's plans were prepared in secret by just a few senior officers in the General's quarters instead of conducting a full staff meeting in the War Room. As to where the spies' information is coming from, that has long been a puzzle."

"Do you have a map of the city and any outlying hills?"

"I can lay my hands on one, sir. What do you propose to do with it?"

"From the top of Gun Hill, I took a compass bearing on the flashing light."

A grunt came from the Sergeant Major.

"Then we have a job to do. If you'll follow me to the

War Room, sir, we'll have a few minutes before General White and General Hunter show up to go over tonight's action."

En route to the one-and-a-half story, wood-frame building that had previously housed a dry goods shop, but was now utilized as General White's Headquarters for planning the defense of Ladysmith, Sergeant Major Toft cautioned the Lieutenant to speak only in a low voice within the building. "In case the walls have somehow grown ears," he explained. "And should we run into anyone there, let me do the talking if you don't mind, sir."

On the porch in front of the door into the Headquarters building, they found their way barred by a sentry with his rifle at Port Arms.

Taking two firm steps forward, the Sergeant Major stuck his face within a few scant inches of the sentry's own.

"Corporal Tommy Atkins is it?" growled the Sergeant Major. "Stopping me from getting into my own Headquarters are you? And you with your uniform out of place. I'll have you on Parade if you're not careful."

"But, Sergeant Major, General White said no one was to enter at night without his say so."

"And was it the General who pulled you out of the line of fire during the Matabele Rebellion? Tell me now, was it also the General who wiped your nose and dusted you off when you were a stumbling private in the Queen's Army and couldn't tell your arse from your pith helmet?"

"No, Sergeant Major."

"Then I think your best response for now is a healthy silence and an empty mind."

Corporal Atkins snapped to attention, eyes straight forward.

Lieutenant Pierce and Sergeant Major Toft passed

through the doorway and over to the war table. Toft sorted through several rolled up maps. When the correct map was selected and stretched out with all four corners weighted down, Pierce plotted a line from Gun Hill along the azimuth of the compass reading he had taken earlier that night. The pencil line crossed several buildings in the city. He mentally added a block wide path on either side of the line to minimize any heading error.

"Note the buildings of interest to yourself," whispered the Sergeant Major, "but we have to leave before the General arrives. Otherwise we'll have a lot of explaining to do in front of other officers, sir, which may not be wise seeing as how we don't know where the leak is as yet. Meanwhile, I'll stand watch at the door."

In his officer's notebook, Lieutenant Pierce scribbled the locations of six buildings that lay along the azimuth as it passed through the city. Finished, he placed his pencil at the side of the table and hurried to roll up the map and restore it to its original position. In his haste, he bumped against the table. His pencil rolled off the edge and fell to the floor. Quickly, he bent over and retrieved it from where it lay on top of a miniature mound of sawdust. Straightening up, he glanced around the room as if to make sure all was still in order.

At the front wall where the entrance door and two large windows overlooked the veranda, Pierce observed Sergeant Major Toft peering out of a slit in one of the front window coverings. To his right and left, Pierce noted several other windows which had originally been set into each of the building's side walls when it was a dry goods store. All of these openings had recently been covered over with army blankets to keep interior light from shining outside, plus to catch any glass shards if the windows happened to shatter. To the rear, Pierce observed an open doorway leading into a small room where a staircase ran up to the attic. The outside door in this small room to the rear appeared locked and bolted from the inside. Glancing up showed Pierce the usual high ceiling built to dissipate the heat during the hot months. All the dry goods, shelves, counters and other equipment had been removed from the main floor, leaving behind only three tables and several wooden chairs.

"Time to go, sir," whispered the Sergeant Major.

Lieutenant Pierce nodded and turned to the door. Together they left the War Room, with the Sergeant Major pausing on the veranda to have a few quiet words with Corporal Atkins before continuing down the street. Near the intersection where the Lieutenant would go his separate way, the Sergeant Major inquired, "Pardon me for asking, sir, but did you find anything?"

"Too early to tell. I'll take a walk around in the morning when the light is better and have a look."

"Very well, sir. Good night."

Continuing on to his quarters, Lieutenant Pierce let his mind run free on the night's happenings out in the South African bush. Inside his private room, he poured water into a large tin bowl and scrubbed the night black soot from his face and hands. Only a few hours left until sunrise. Loosening his tunic collar, but keeping his uniform on, Pierce stretched out on his campaign cot and closed his eyes. No use. Adrenaline still flowing from earlier events kept any restful sleep at bay. Half dreams crept into his head of bushy faced Boers, Mauser rifles aimed from cover in the night, distant lights flashing code in Dutch, and...

He awoke to the sound of a bugle. His coming thought at the end of the dream hadn't fully formed yet. Like morning mist on sunlit waters, it slowly evaporated. He lay on the cot a few minutes more, trying to bring back the thought in his dream.

Finally giving up, he arose for the day's tasks, shaved and set out for his walk. Notes in hand, he followed the general path he'd plotted on the War Room map the night before, looking at buildings on both sides of the azimuth to allow for any compass inaccuracies. Some buildings were automatically rejected since their line of sight to Gun Hill was blocked by taller buildings. It was the taller buildings he found to be of interest. He jotted down locations and descriptions of three tall, wood-constructed buildings that intrigued him the most. And then the elusive thought from morning dreams began to take form again.

Questions buzzed in his head.

An idea grew.

Since the usual daily bombardment hadn't moved to this part of the city yet, he reversed direction and headed for the parade ground. Along the edge of the parade field, he found a squad of soldiers marching across the brown un-watered grass. Their flickering eyes and distracted movements made them appear ready to bolt at a moment's notice.

Their Sergeant, sporting a heavily waxed mustache and barking his commands in a thick Highlands accent, kept turning his head slightly toward any booming sounds coming in from the surrounding hills while drilling his squad of misfits on the short grass square. At Pierce's approach, the Sergeant snapped to attention and saluted.

Pierce returned the salute and inquired, "Where might I find the Sergeant Major?"

"He's overseeing positioning of the long range naval guns brought in by ox trains last night while some of the lads distracted the Boer with that raid, sir. Try the south wall."

As he left the Parade Ground, Pierce heard the whistle of an incoming artillery round passing off to one side, followed by the commanding voice of the Sergeant. "Stand fast, lads. We're not finished with our drill yet. You still owe me five more minutes. Won't do to come up short now."

Halfway to the southern wall and keeping an ear out for any change in the artillery barrage, Pierce rounded the corner of a house in the civilian section. Something immediately smacked into his legs below the knee. Having not heard any stray rounds, Piece looked down in surprise.

"Sorry, sir," said a young voice. "Didn't know anyone was coming."

A worn soccer ball bounced off the side of the house and rolled into the street. Right behind the ball, a young boy of six scooped it up before it could travel any farther.

"Why aren't you in the shelters?" demanded Pierce.

The boy wiped his nose on his shirt sleeve.

"There's nothing to do there except sit all day. I wanted to play in the fresh air so I snuck out."

"Where's your parents?"

"Me Mom's helping with wounded in the hospital and me Da's soldiering in one of the trenches."

"Who's watching over you?"

"Nobody, I don't need no watching."

Lieutenant Pierce made a shooing motion with his hand.

"Get on back to one of the shelters before you get hurt."

The boy gave an impish grin.

"I see you walking around out here."

"That's because I've got a job to do."

"Ha," replied the boy, "me Da says that if everyone

done their job like he's doing, then this would all be over in no time and I wouldn't have no trouble playing outside."

Pierce took two quick steps forward.

Clutching the ball under his arm, the boy ran. Two blocks later, he stopped and looked back over his shoulder. Then he nonchalantly dropped the ball to the ground and started kicking it away up the street.

With scarce time for distractions, Pierce watched him go before moving on himself. Along the southern entrenchments, he found Sergeant Major Toft observing the laying of four naval guns carted in from a battleship off the coast. Several artillery officers and observers seemed to be making their final adjustments before returning the Boer fire.

"I have some questions," Pierce began.

The Sergeant Major kept his gaze on the recently placed naval cannon.

"Ask away, sir."

"Tell me about the building that General White is using as his headquarters."

"Well, sir, it was a dry goods store owned by a man who left Ladysmith shortly after hostilities began. Since the building was already vacated, one of the city fathers suggested there would be no problem with our using it. As the store's outside walls consisted of stone, the building would survive anything except a direct hit; therefore it suited our purposes quite well. The main floor was mostly empty when we took over."

"And up the stairs, what's in the attic?"

"Well, sir, we was told the owner moved all his store counters, shelves and personal goods up there for safe keeping until the war was over. Since the attic door was locked, well boarded up and had a personal seal on it, we couldn't get in without a lot of effort and destruction to the doorway. The General decided he didn't want any war claims from civilians for unnecessary damage, or potential charges of pilfering, so we let it be. Why do you ask, sir?"

"When I dropped my pencil on the floor, it landed in a small pile of sawdust. Not the rough type of sawdust someone might scatter on the floor to absorb spillage. No, this was a fine, light sawdust that might come from drilling a hole in a board. In fact, I noticed a couple of these small piles of sawdust in different parts of the room, mostly in out of the way places where boots hadn't yet trampled the piles flat."

"Small piles of sawdust, sir?"

"Correct."

"In various places on the floor?"

"Right. And there was a slight film of sawdust coating parts of the War Room map table.

"Are you saying, sir, that someone is hiding up in the attic, boring holes in the ceiling in order to keep a watch on the General's plans?"

"I'm saying that we ought to take a look and find out."

The Sergeant Major "humphed" once as he maintained his gaze on activity around the naval guns. His hands were clasped behind his back as if at Parade Rest. Lieutenant Pierce had almost given up hope of receiving an answer to his proposal when Toft suddenly bellowed at a passing private. The private came on the run.

"Listen up, lad. Roll Corporal Tommy Atkins out of his cot. Tell him to bring six good men with rifles and a couple of crowbars to meet me outside the Headquarters building. Tell the Corporal no fuss, mind you. I want this on the quiet. Now be off."

The private disappeared toward the barracks.

"You have your sidearm with you, sir?"

"I do."

"Then perhaps we should take a stroll in that direction. It being almost noon, the officers will be at mess and we shan't disturb any planning sessions."

Now realizing that he'd had nothing to eat since the evening before and would very well miss out on the noon meal as well, the Lieutenant felt the first pangs of hunger. No matter, they'd have to wait.

Approaching the Headquarters building, Toft made comment. "I should warn you, sir, that if we find nothing in the attic, then jokes will soon be making the rounds that a certain Lieutenant Pierce has bats in his belfry and sawdust for brains. No offense intended, sir."

"None taken, Sergeant Major. But since I see your Corporal already has his men drawn up at the side of the building it's a moot point, there's no turning back now."

"As you wish, sir."

The Sergeant Major gave his orders in a quiet voice, then turned to the Lieutenant.

"Sir, if you'll be so kind as to go inside and unlock the rear door, I'll take the men around back and you can let us in."

Nodding his agreement, Lieutenant Pierce climbed the stairs onto the veranda, strode past the day sentry with no trouble and entered the front door. No one in the room. Unhurriedly, as if he were merely there to pick up some reports, the Lieutenant gradually made his way to the rear of the building and unbolted the back door. Eight armed men filed silently into the back room and waited at the bottom of the staircase.

The Sergeant Major pointed out two soldiers with crowbars and motioned them up the steps.

"The lads will work fast, sir, but if anyone is up there, he'll know we're coming. I just don't want to give him too long to think about his options."

Nails screeched as boards were pulled off the attic door frame. One soldier yanked the last board out of the passage and threw it down the stairs. The other pried a hefty lock off its hasp, breaking the wax seal loose from the door. Then he jammed one end of the metal pry bar between the door and its frame and muscled the wood apart. Quickly, he flattened his back against the stair wall. The other five soldiers, with Lieutenant Pierce and the Sergeant Major among them, rushed up the last few stairs. As the door crashed inward, a shot rang out from the attic. One of the lead soldiers clutched his side and fell backward. Corporal Atkins and a nearby private leaned into the upper room and fired their rifles. Lieutenant Pierce tried to see in, but the doorway was now jammed by soldiers pushing and crowding into the attic. Another shot sounded from inside the upper room. Then those at the top of the stairs grew quiet.

"Step aside, lads, and let me have a look," ordered the Sergeant Major.

"He shot himself," murmured the Corporal.

"I expect so," replied the senior NCO. "The thought of facing the hangman for spying probably didn't appeal to him. Now go fetch the doctor and an ambulance wagon for our own wounded man."

Lieutenant Pierce forced his way into the attic. Crates of food and barrels of water were stacked on the floor around the inside slope of the rafters. A campaign table and an overturned camp stool sat in the middle of the room. On top of the table rested a bulls-eye lantern and several handwritten pages. In a heap on the floor near one of the table legs lay a bearded man of medium build. A pistol hung from one finger on his right hand.

"Well, sir," said the Sergeant Major, "We won't get

much out of him now, but it was good work on your part just the same. It would appear you got our spy."

In silence, Lieutenant Pierce leafed through the handwritten papers and studied the lantern. A piece was missing here. He glanced out the small windows under the peak of the roof at either end of the long attic. Neither window faced in the direction of Gun Hill. Next, he searched through the pockets of the dead Boer. A tobacco pouch, small clay pipe and a photo of a large Boer family in front of their farm house. Nothing for intelligence here... but he felt they had only found one of the spies.

Boots approached.

"If we're done here, sir, I'll have the lads drag the body out and clean up before the officers return."

Pierce contemplated the lantern on the table.

"On the contrary, Sergeant Major. Have Corporal Atkins cover the body with a blanket, then the Corporal will arrange that none of these soldiers leave the attic until further notice. You yourself will proceed to the dispensary with the doctor and our wounded man. Stay only long enough to set a guard on the hospital room. Ensure that no one speaks about our actions in the attic. When you have finished with their sequestering--quarantine them if you have to--you will return to me forthwith. I may have a plan in mind for tonight."

"Yes, sir. And as to the General and any questions he might have?"

"I will explain everything to him upon his return. I expect this building and anyone in it will then also be subject to a quarantine of silence."

As another moonless night settled down over the South African hills, the garrison at Ladysmith went dark. Up in the attic above Commanding General Sir George Stewart White's Headquarters, Lieutenant Pierce positioned a Signals Officer at the small windows at each end of the long room. Both Signals Officers had a bullseye lantern ready in hand.

Blackout blankets had been hung up in the center of the attic, surrounding the table where Lieutenant Pierce and the Sergeant Major had laid out a map of the city and the encircling hills. On this map, the thin pencil line, drawn from Gun Hill to the City of Ladysmith on the previous night, laid an accusing mark across the top of several buildings.

"According to this line, I expect to find our answer in one of the tall buildings behind our Headquarters," Lieutenant Pierce explained to General White. "However, I have placed signal lanterns at each end of our building just in case."

"And then?" inquired the General.

"Well, sir, we don't know if the Boers have a prearranged time set for communications, but based on my observations at Gun Hill last night, we do know they have previously communicated just before midnight. So, at the mark of every hour, each of our two Signals Officers will blink a distress signal in Dutch out of his window. It's my hope that the other spy in the city will assume his comrade has suffered some illness or accident and therefore will give a reply. That should give us the other spy's location."

"I'm getting a series of lantern flashes," interrupted the Signals Officer stationed at the rear attic window. "It's coming from the steeple of the old Dutch Reformed Church, but that's supposed to have been closed up when the Boers departed the city before hostilities began."

"Can you read the message?" asked the Lieutenant.

"No, it must be in Dutch. What do you want me to do?"

"Keep sending the distress signal, but slowly as if

you're having trouble sending. We need to keep whoever it is there for a couple more minutes."

As a squad of soldiers thundered down the rear staircase en route to the church, Lieutenant Pierce could hear the Sergeant Major's encouraging voice.

"Corporal Atkins, do this right and there may be a sergeant's stripes in it for you yet. Lively now lads, lively, we've work to do. Oom Paul and the Boer never rest, and neither can we. See if you can take this one alive."

Lieutenant Pierce pulled out his pocket watch and anxiously watched the second hand move around the dial. One minute passed, then two.

A cry came from the British Signals Officer stationed at the rear of the attic. "The lantern in the church steeple has broken off in mid-signal, sir."

"Keep sending," ordered Pierce. He'd heard no shots, maybe they'd get lucky.

The second hand on his pocket watch swept around three more full circles.

"Still no reply, sir."

"Cease operation," replied Lieutenant Pierce. "By now it's already been decided one way or the other."

He turned to the General. "With your permission, sir."

"Good work, Lieutenant. Go on."

Pierce rushed down the stairs in time to meet a breathless Private coming in the rear door of the Headquarters building.

"Corporal Atkins sent me, sir. We caught the other spy in the church tower. He's a Dutchman, one of the city's shopkeepers that stayed behind during the evacuation. Right now he's singing like a lark. We should be able to round up a couple more conspirators. The Sergeant Major sends his compliments."

Lieutenant Pierce allowed himself a slight smile. Two

spies caught that they knew about, but how many more still operated inside the defenses of Ladysmith?

The Sergeant Major had been correct in his comments. Oom Paul, or Uncle Paul, as the Boers called their President, did indeed have very long ears, many of them right here within the encampment. There'd be no rest for anyone in Ladysmith until General Buller's relief column arrived from the Tugela River crossing to raise the siege.

Pierce checked his pocket watch again. Two more hours of quiet left before the Boers greeted the morning sunrise with their usual cannon fire. The city could sleep peacefully for a while. They'd not be hearing from Long Tom this day or any day soon, yet there would be little sleep for himself. He'd find a way to cope. Then, he wondered how the young boy with the soccer ball would fare in the days to come. Wars, it seemed, had a habit of dragging on and on.

ON THE PERFUME RIVER

"One week shore leave," agreed the Captain, "but only because the ship is down for repairs. No more time than that."

I figured one week was long enough to take care of my business. According to the date on the letter in my shirt pocket, I was probably too late getting here anyway. By now, the problem should have been solved, and done so without my assistance. I could drop in on my French cousin, say hello and be back to the *S.S. Pedang* with several days to spare.

"One more item, Mister Regret," continued the Captain. "At the end of the week, this ship will raise anchor and sail for Singapore with or without benefit of First Mate."

His meaning was clear. If I wasn't back onboard in time, then I'd find myself stranded on the beach in French Indo-China, looking for a berth on some other South Seas freighter. But I didn't see that as being a problem, since my little family visit would only take a couple of days at most.

One of the obliging East African deckhands rowed me ashore at the mouth of the Song Huong River, the one the French call "The Perfume River" from the aroma of all the flowers growing along both banks farther inland from the sea. If that were true, then it would be one of the few lowland rivers in Southeast Asia without that hot musty smell. Guess I'd be finding out real soon.

The East African tossed my sea bag high up onto the beach in the hot golden sand. In return, I turned the nose of the dinghy around and gave it a push back out into the South China Sea. He flashed a wide grin, showing off his white teeth, but was too busy rowing to spare me any other farewell.

A short hike brought me to one of the two large salt lagoons just in from the sand dunes at the river's entrance. Here, my halting Cajun French and a silver American quarter soon bought the services of a pole-powered sampan for the nine mile ride upriver to Hue, the capital of Annam. Tonkin to the north, Annam in the middle and Cochinchina to the south being the three states that made up the thousand mile curve of coast land running south from Kwang-si Province in China down to the Gulf of Siam. France had won this colonial federation in the Franco-Chinese War fifteen years earlier. Then the Annamese quickly found they had only exchanged one conqueror for another, while many of the Chinese had remained behind as wealthy businessmen with great influence on the local economy. And now, with the current unrest and nationalist uprisings in their two northern states, the French were suspicious of any strangers.

I paid the boatman, stepped up onto the dock on the left bank of the river and shouldered my sea bag. When I turned around, a gendarme in khaki uniform and white pith helmet was waiting for me.

"Your papers, monsieur."

I handed them over and waited silently while he struggled to read through my documents.

"Monsieur Paul Regret, why you come to Hue from America?"

Since my Cajun French had to be better than his broken English, I switched over to his mother tongue.

"My cargo ship is being repaired downriver at Thuan An, so I thought I'd visit my second cousin who lives here in the city."

"And who is your cousin?"

"Jean LeDuc. His father owns a tea farm up the river."

At the mention of Jean's name, I'd noticed a quick glance from the gendarme's eyes, but he said nothing about my statement. Still, my insatiable curiosity inclined me to pry.

"You searching for someone in particular?"

The gendarme dropped his gaze back to my documents.

"The colonies seem to be getting a few gun runners and mercenaries these days," he replied in a gruff manner.

Returning my papers, he waved me on my way. Now he seemed to be in a sudden hurry to go somewhere. Within a few steps, he'd disappeared into the crowd of Chinese coolies and Annamese laborers loading boxes and bundles from the dock onto horse-drawn carts or onto the ends of carrying poles lying across the shoulders of other workers. Only the bobbing of the gendarme's white European pith helmet above the mass of oriental people and their straw-colored conical hats showed which way he'd gone. My business took me in the same direction, only at a slower pace in the tropical heat. I had been many things in my time, but this was the first time I'd been mistaken for a gun smuggler.

Waiting street side at the end of the dock rested a cyclopousse, the French term for a three-wheeled passenger vehicle pedaled from behind by the rear half of a bicycle. Several of these cycle machines sat nearby, but this one in particular stood closest to the curb, separated from the rest of the cyclos as if it were this driver's turn to pick up a passenger. The other operators looked on with sullen faces.

For a small fee, this half naked cyclo driver, wearing only a long black loin cloth knotted around his waist and one of those straw-colored conical hats of woven palm fronds, pedaled me two blocks into the city to a small hotel of his recommendation. From outside on the cobblestone pavement, Madame Pho's didn't look like much, just a lobby with a small room on the ground floor where the old concierge lived, and a nearby stairway leading up. All the flavor of a second class establishment for foreigners who couldn't afford the high society places. Fortunately, all the rooms for boarders were up on the second floor to catch any available breeze. A definite advantage in this heat and humidity. Plus, the open air windows of rooms on the front side overlooked the busy traffic down on the street. One could keep an eye on the world outside.

Dropping my sea bag onto the bed in my room, I locked the door and returned to the lobby downstairs. The same cyclo driver who had brought me from the river docks now grinned and waved me over. Looked like he'd attached himself to me. No doubt the silver coins in my pocket had something to do with it.

For the next two days, I tried to find my cousin. His return address on the letter turned out to be one of the fancier hotels in the city. It could have been my common appearance, but I didn't find the staff at this hotel to be very friendly. The clerk at the registration book finally deigned to look down his nose at me after I'd stood waiting for ten minutes in front of his teak-wood counter that continued to lack customers other than myself.

"Jean LeDuc?" I inquired.

A long cold stare in silence was his immediate answer.

"Monsieur LeDuc left several days ago without notifying us," came the clerk's second response to my appearance, "and he has not yet returned. Thus his account is now closed and his personal belongings have been removed to the manager's office."

Not paying his own way didn't sound like my cousin, but it had been a couple of years since I'd last seen him. Even though we had once been close companions, maybe he'd changed during that time.

The clerk continued. "Since you seem to have some acquaintance with Monsieur LeDuc, do you wish to pay his bill?"

Declining to make that offer, I asked to see Jean's belongings and was haughtily informed such a thing would not be possible. The management would simply not allow it.

A quick glance in all directions assured me the lobby was completely empty, no customers or bell boys in sight. The clerk had the front desk all to himself for the moment. I stepped around the registration counter and backed the clerk against the wall.

It could have been the hard look in my eyes, but I rather suspect it was the sight of the knife scar on my left cheek that persuaded him to come across. The clerk now quickly told a different story. According to him, someone had broken into the manager's office during the previous night and removed all of Monsieur LeDuc's articles. The clerk further claimed that he, himself, had no wish to point fingers at any suspect, but strongly implied it had been Jean himself, as Jean's account had been overdue long before his disappearance. When I left, the clerk was straightening out the wrinkles in his white shirt front.

With my cyclo driver now pointing the way from his bicycle seat behind me, I tried several other hotels. No one with the name LeDuc had been registered. Two choices remained; find my way upriver to his father's tea farm and see what the family knew, or return to the ship and forget the whole thing.

My mind kept going back to his letter. He'd said he was about to make his fortune on his own, but needed a man he could trust to watch his back. The rest of the letter was fanciful dribble about Mandarin gold and river pirates that he would explain all about later when I arrived. As compensation for my assistance, he offered me a share of what he had already obtained and hidden away, but I was to hurry because he believed he was now in some danger.

He'd probably hoped to whet my interest with the latter statement and to some degree he had. Who wouldn't be interested in getting their mitts on some Chinese gold and having a little adventure to go with it? Too bad the mail had been so slow catching up with our ship. Now Jean was gone and I'd never know what this escapade had really been about.

Arriving back at Madame Pho's as dark clouds rolled up in the evening sky, I dismissed the cyclo driver, then hurried a few steps along the street to approach a food vendor calling out his wares. A long curved carrying pole balanced the vendor's two large yellow baskets, one at each end. He removed the pole from his shoulder and gently deposited his load on the sidewalk. Dropping himself into a flat-footed squat with the backs of his thighs resting on his calf muscles, he pulled a short wooden stool out of one of the baskets and placed it on the sidewalk for me to sit on.

We agreed on a price. He handed me a pair of chopsticks and a bowl of cooked rice. With a large metal spoon, he ladled vegetables and some kind of meat over my rice. His pidgin-French left me wondering what type of animal the meat had come from, however, I did recognize chopped green onions, tomato pieces and brown soy sauce in the rest of the mixture. While he waited for me to finish eating, he smoked a hand-rolled cigarette and tried to carry on with our fragmented conversation. He grinned a lot, but I couldn't figure out half of what he was saying.

Through the food vendor's haze of cigarette smoke, I noticed an elderly Annamese man cross the street toward Madame Pho's. When the old man, dressed in the worker's usual black glossy cotton pants and long sleeve shirt of the same material, caught me watching, he quickly ducked his head and disappeared into Madame Pho's lobby. I was pretty sure I'd seen the fellow hanging around on the street outside my hotel for the last couple of days. Twice before, I'd had the feeling of being watched by someone, but whenever I turned in his direction, he seemed to have just then looked away. If I approached, he melted into the crowd. One of these days, I would come up on his blind side and find out his interest in my personal business.

But then I also suspected that his weren't the only eyes whose presence I felt. Most of the time I put these feelings off to my six foot stature walking around in a five foot native world.

Done with my meal, I returned the bowl and chopsticks to the food vendor. He was washing them in a container of water in one of the baskets when I walked away into the gathering night. To brighten the darkness, shopkeepers began to light colored lanterns hanging outside their stores.

At the doorway to Madame Pho's, I looked for the concierge at his usual post. No one was visible in the small lobby and no one appeared on the stairs, yet his lanterns had been lit. I wanted to ask about the old man who'd come in, but no luck here. Continuing up the stairs, I moved down the hallway to my room.

With the key in one hand, I placed my other palm against the wooden door. Before I could insert key in lock, the door swung partway open. Light spilling in from the hallway showed me the soles of two sandals, toes down, at the end of a pair of black pant legs. Whoever was stretched out on my floor in that position had to have trouble breathing through a bent nose...if he was breathing at all. Pushing the door wider to admit more light, I also instinctively took a step backward and drew a sailor's knife from the sheath at my waist.

A dart whistled out of the receding shadows in the room and stuck in the door, followed by a rustling sound as a small shape in the dim interior leaped onto the windowsill, dropped outside and was gone. I rushed to the window, but the intruder had vanished like a black cat into the night.

Returning to the door, I closed it and struck a match. The body on my floor was the Annamese I'd seen entering Madame Pho's while I was eating supper with the food vendor. With a flare of light, the match burned quickly and went out, leaving the room in darkness. Striking the next match, I lit the lantern, but kept the wick trimmed low and the lantern close to the floor. No sense lighting up the interior of my room for other watchers to see inside.

Upon examining the old man, I found a dart clutched in his right hand and a slight trickle of blood trailing down from the right side of his neck. A second dart was lodged between his shoulder blades where he couldn't get at it. To my knowledge, the savage hill tribes up in the Blue Mountains used crossbows, not blow pipes for their killing. This assassin was more likely to be from one of the South Sea Islands and used a deadly snake poison on his darts. Someone with access to foreign ports had evidently imported his own personal killer. A few inches closer and that third dart could've been in me instead of the door. The question was why me at all?

Underneath the body, I discovered a small mahogany box in the victim's left hand. The old Annamese fellow must have fallen on it and the killer hadn't enough time to thoroughly search the body before he heard me coming up the stairs. I opened the lid. The box was empty. Maybe the assassin had already taken its contents. I tossed the box on top of the bed covers and turned out the lantern.

Now the problem was getting rid of the corpse. A quick check out in the hallway showed an empty corridor. Luckily, the old man didn't weigh much and it was a short carry to an open hall window overlooking the alley. A muffled thud in the soft dirt and trash out back marked the end of his short downward journey. All three poisoned darts went with him. No witnesses, no evidence, no immediate problem.

Back in the room, I locked the door and wedged a chair under the handle. With the lantern re-lit, I sat on the bed and turned the box over in my hands. It seemed constructed of several pieces of smoothly polished wood. But, there on the bottom of this small wooden container, someone had carved my cousin's name.

Thoughts rushed to my mind. Why did the elderly Annamese have the box in the first place? What brought him to his death in my room? And who wanted to kill him, and now me? If there were to be any answers, it appeared I'd have to find them on my own. The old man obviously wasn't up to taking questions.

I rotated the box again. This little wooden container reminded me of the toy puzzle boxes I'd brought back from one of my trips to Shanghai as presents for my sister's kids in New Orleans. Push on the right piece of wood and the interlocking parts revealed a secret compartment. Three of my pushes later, a section of wood slid noiselessly to one side. Another push on a different piece and a small drawer sprang out from the front. Inside, laid a folded piece of paper. I opened it and read.

> The messenger is my friend. Gold bought his services.
> Is there time yet for you to arrive?
> In speed lies our safety. The river is the path.
> Royal is our reward. Grave is our danger.
> ~Jean

The best I could figure out, he wanted me to take a trip upriver. Any other purpose in the message had to be some kind of code. Logic said he must be hiding out at his folk's tea farm and had sent the old Annamese to fetch me. Fine, I'd take one more day of my shore leave, then catch a sampan back to the *S.S. Pedang* before it sailed.

But if someone were willing to kill over a mahogany box which contained only a paper message, then some precautions were necessary to hide the message until I had a chance to determine its full meaning. All I needed was a way.

An extra square of cloth, made from the same material as my sailor shirt, rested in my kit bag. It would probably do the trick. I laboriously copied the message with India ink, one sentence per line onto the cloth. Then I sewed the square onto the tail of my shirt, message side down, as if it were a patch job to cover a hole in the garment. Next, the original paper message burst into flames, much like a moth turned to ashes, on the inside of the lamp. Finished with all I could do for now, I turned the lantern off and sought the peace of sleep. Outside on the street, noise dropped to a mere whisper, but my thoughts wouldn't rest. Dead men and gold coins flitted through my dreams.

In the morning, the lobby of Madame Pho's was quiet. There'd been no hue and cry about any body found in the alley, and I didn't want to be the first to inquire.

Out at the curb rested my usual cyclo driver as if he'd spent the night waiting for me. Luckily by chance, he knew just the boat to take me upriver. Instead of a pole-powered sampan which would take a long time for the trip, he had a friend with a steam engine launch that could move fast in these waters. If we hurried, the friend should still be at the Hue docks. Fine by me. I tossed him a silver dime and we were off.

At the docks, my driver pointed out a hundred foot launch with huge eyes painted on each side of the prow, a dragon boat. From what I'd heard during my short time here, the eyes helped the boat to see at night and in bad waters. It was one superstition that a sailor like me could well understand.

The steam engine was already running when I stepped aboard. But before I even met the captain or haggled about a fee, the ropes were cast off from the dock and the launch started upriver. Two other images immediately came to mind. The French gendarme from three days ago at the dock, appeared to be waving frantically at me and shouting something I couldn't quite hear across the water and above the noise of the engine. And secondly, for some reason my cyclo driver had come aboard with me. Now, he no longer seemed to be the simple, grinning street operator out for a few silver coins pedaling tourists around the city.

From the stern of the launch, a large Malay, bare-chested, with a wicked knife in his belt and a wide yellow cloth tied around his forehead, came forward with a bundle of clothes to help my cyclo driver dress. The driver exchanged his knotted loin cloth for a pair of *Cai-quan*, black silk pants, and a black *Ao-dai*, an ankle-length, long-sleeved silk tunic split up both sides to the waist. The conical hat came off his head and was replaced with a black turban-like hat open in the middle, which left the hair showing on the top of his head and let out the tropical heat.

I had it in mind to leap over the side and take my chances swimming for shore. Of course, the two Annamese guys, dressed in old French army jackets and conical straw hats, coming out of the cabin with bolt action rifles at the ready had other ideas. These two river pirates had enough ammunition in the bandoliers slung across their shoulders to shoot all day at anyone who might suddenly decide to go swimming in the river.

The other thing that kept me from diving overboard was the beautiful Eurasian female who stepped out behind the two guards. Dressed in white silk pants and a blood red *ao-dai*, she had a light tan complexion to her face, long sleek black hair, pale-green jade earrings, an elaborate jade necklace around her slender neck and a couple of 24K gold rings on her fingers. I would have been in love if it hadn't been for the revolver in her dainty hands. But, regardless of the gun's presence, I felt a strong attraction to the soft lilt in her voice.

"Monsieur Regret, we have been waiting for you."

I almost kissed her hand in the French way of greeting a lady, but there was the small obstacle of that pistol between us.

"You have the advantage on me, Madame," was the best I could come up with on short notice. "Who are you?"

"Many refer to me as the Queen of the River. Others know me as the Jade Princess or Lady Thi Ne. In my business, I have many names."

"What exactly is your business?"

The corners of her mouth curled slightly.

"Businessmen in the cities, farmers in the countryside and people on the river pay me for protection."

"From what?"

Her eyes sparkled and she almost smiled.

"From river pirates."

This was starting to sound like the same racket a couple of Black Hand fellows I knew were pulling on local business people back in New Orleans. Extortion, kidnapping and ransom headed up their game. The only difference here seemed to be the lady had a prettier face than those mugs did. I had no doubt the results came out the same.

Then I had another thought.

"You said you were waiting for me."

"Yes, but before we continue our discussion, I wish to have the message the old man brought to your room."

I shrugged and gave her my best grin.

"The old man was dead when I entered the room. He said nothing and he handed me nothing."

The Jade Princess raised her pistol to the level of my

stomach.

"Search him," she said.

The large Malay with the yellow cloth around his head ambled over behind me. He turned out my pockets, felt through my clothes and took my sailor's knife. When he finally stepped off to one side, he slowly shook his head sideways to signify I had nothing of importance on me. She lowered her pistol.

"I am a business woman," she said after a moment. "Perhaps you will take tea with me in front of the cabin?"

Right now I could've used a strong whiskey, or some of that local beer whose hangover made you feel like you had one ball bearing rolling around in your skull. But, even tea was better than what I probably could have expected under the circumstances, so I nodded in agreement.

At a table set up on the deck forward of the cabin, I noticed there were only two cups made of fine china and two saucers to match. Looked like my now dressed up cyclo driver wasn't invited to this tea party, but then he seemed to be pretty busy giving orders to the crew members. Definitely not the earlier image of servility he'd presented to me during the last three days in Hue.

My gaze also took in the four smooth-bore cannons concealed under canvas tarps and beneath piles of woven baskets on the fore deck. Whether she was fending off rival pirates or boarding a merchant's ship, this lady obviously had a deadly edge in her chosen profession. Another time, I could have taken pleasure in the perfumed air floating in from the vast fields of red and yellow flowers passing by on both banks, or maybe even enjoyed the sight of the few majestic nearby tombs where Annamite emperors had been interred after their death. But with the current situation I'd have to tread carefully to ensure my survival.

The Malay poured tea, then stood directly behind me. I hadn't seen where Lady Thi Ne had placed her pistol, but assumed it was close by.

"Let me explain," she began, "and then we will negotiate. Your cousin, Jean LeDuc, sought me out several days past. He claimed to know where the Chinese Governor of Hue hid the treasury just before the French Navy destroyed the Chinese Armada in the great battle fifteen years ago. According to Monsieur LeDuc, he learned this secret from the lips of a dying man who had helped conceal the Mandarin gold."

"Why did he come to you?" I inquired.

"The treasure is heavy, the risks are great and I control the river."

"How do you know he actually found it?"

She nodded to the Malay. He opened a small, red-lacquered chest that sat near her slippered feet. On the table top, he then laid two bars of soft yellow gold and a small golden statue of a Chinese lion, a replica of the ones that guard temple gates and the palaces of Oriental emperors. The statue was a work of art, and the gold bars were of such a high purity that I could scratch them with my thumbnail.

"Monsieur LeDuc gave me these three items as a good faith payment to help him recover and safely transport the remainder."

"Why haven't you already done so?"

"Your cousin wished to wait for your arrival to help cover his back, as he put it. He would not divulge the location until he felt ready to go forward. In the meantime, he was kidnapped by one of my rivals, a Chinese Mandarin by the name of Cheng Shih. Cheng had been an official in the old Governor's cabinet, but he knew only rumors of the treasury's hidden location. Unfortunately for Cheng, your cousin did not stand up well to torture, his heart evidently collapsed. We later found his body in the river."

Suddenly, this drinking of tea didn't seem to be the proper action to be doing at the moment.

"How will I recognize this Cheng Shih?" I asked. "I may wish to have a talk with him about the manner of my cousin's departure."

The Lady Thi Ne gave me a description of the Mandarin and concluded with the tattoo inked on his left forearm. "It is a dragon with the tail starting at the man's elbow and the dragon's head stretching out onto the back of the Mandarin's hand. You can see this tattoo when the sleeve of his gown is pulled back."

I grimly thanked her for the information.

"Don't be too hasty in your appreciation," she responded. "We have yet to conclude our own negotiations."

"Go on," I said.

"Before your cousin disappeared, he gave a message to the old Annamese man you later found in your room, and instructed him to wait at the Hue docks for your arrival. We did not know what was in this message. That's when I stationed my lieutenant, Nguyen Van Hoac, as a cyclo driver to keep an eye on events as they unfolded. The French gendarme you met at the docks is in my pay and told me when you appeared in Hue. Unfortunately, he also sells information to my rival, Cheng Shih, so I decided to wait and see what else would happen."

"Then you know the old man was killed by a poison dart before I got to my room, and you know the killer escaped."

"I do." She clapped her hands twice.

I heard movement behind me and turned to see two other river pirates dragging a small man between them.

Their prisoner had the appearance of a jungle savage from one of the more remote Filipino Islands or maybe from the scattered Indonesian backwaters I'd heard about, where white men seldom tread unless they were on the run from the long reach of government officials or some criminal organization. This small tribesman wore a simple loincloth and his long hair was black and matted. Other than that, he slumped in his captors' grasp. The reason was quickly apparent. His entire body had the look of a man who had suffered a sudden uncontrollable seizure while shaving with a straight razor. I had a pretty good idea the Jade Princess was showing me a sample of her handiwork.

"This is the assassin that killed the old man. He works for Cheng Shih and he sought to discover the message your cousin had sent. As you can see, the killer has told us little. Perhaps he doesn't know much, but by tomorrow, he will no longer be of use to me."

She waved her hand and the two guards dragged their half-dead captive away. Half my mind focused on the Jade Princess, the other half listened for an expected telltale splash off the stern of the launch.

"We know you found and read the message," she continued. "My man on the roof across the street from Madame Pho's saw you open the puzzle box and take out a piece of paper. He could not see what you did for a while afterwards, but he did observe when you burned the paper in the lantern. If the message is now secured in your head, then I have a man in my employ that will gladly help you to remember what it said."

At this point, I figured we were pretty well done with the tea party. I had some choices to make and didn't much like any of them. Giving up gold that had never been mine in the first place would be comparatively easy, but I planned to set a high price if I ended up selling my life to these river pirates. I held out my hand.

"Can I have my knife back?"

Lady Thi Ne nodded to the Malay. He laid my knife on the table. When I picked it up, I noticed the revolver had now reappeared in the Lady's hand. She watched my movements closely as I pulled out my shirt tail and began cutting the threads to the cloth patch I'd sewn on the night before. The patch came away in a few short strokes of the blade. I threw the cloth onto the table.

"What is this?"

I flipped the cloth square over so she could see the hand writing on the hidden side.

She read the seven sentences, then glanced up with a frown on her face.

"I copied it word for word," I said. "Maybe you can determine what my cousin meant by his cryptic note."

At the moment she smoothed the square of cloth over the table top to read the words again, I glanced at the way I had rewritten the sentences. And even though the wording was upside down, I now had a clue to the meaning of the note. The answer was quite simple.

"You mentioned the possibility of negotiations between us," I ventured.

She raised her eyes to mine.

"Yes?"

I took my chance.

"If I decipher my cousin's words, what can I expect from you?"

Lady Thi Ne leaned back in her chair and contemplated my question.

"My prior arrangement was with your cousin, not with you. You now expect a share of the Mandarin's treasury?"

I shook my head.

"At this point, I wish only my freedom in order to avenge Jean's death. Any generosity you feel toward me after you locate the Chinese gold is up to you."

She sat quiet for a long time. Then, transferring the revolver to her left hand, she reached out with the fingers of her right and gently traced the scar on my cheek.

"You have a handsome face. It would be a pity to put another mark on it. Tell me the meaning."

"Do we have a deal?" I asked.

"Yes."

"In America we shake hands to seal an agreement."

The Lady hesitated for a heartbeat, then slid her warm right hand on top of my calloused palm. Too bad she still held that pistol.

I shook her hand.

"Read the first word of every sentence," I said. "That will tell you where to look."

She snatched up the cloth square.

"Ah, yes, the Royal Tombs. I see it now. However there is more than one tomb to search and we must avoid detection. This will take some time."

Pushing back her chair, she stood and gave orders to the crew. The launch now turned toward a fleet of sampans along the shore where a smaller river fed into the Perfume.

"What about me?" I inquired.

"You will be our guest until our business is concluded."

The engine of the launch cut down to idle as the Malay tied us up to one of the sampans in the fleet. My ex-cyclo driver, now dressed like an Annamese gentleman, came forward and motioned me over into the waiting sampan.

"Have no fear," he said. "The Jade Princess almost always keeps her bargains." Then he gave orders to the black pajamaed river pirates in the sampan. The launch cast off and headed back downriver.

This new band of cutthroats, with me in their custody, poled our boat a short way up the tributary where we stayed in a small villa for several days. I could keep my sailor knife, but they evidently had orders not to speak with me. As long as I stayed within the walls, there seemed to be no problem. They supplied drink and cooked food and otherwise left me to my own. Alone, in the quiet hours, I often pictured the face and slender form of the lady pirate in her white silk pants and blood red *ao-dai*. Perhaps we would meet again.

Then one morning, the guards failed to bring my breakfast. The villa felt empty. On a small table near the front door, I found the red lacquered chest from our tea party on the launch. Inside were two small bars of soft gold and the miniature golden statue of a Chinese lion. My cousin's good faith gesture to the Jade Princess, the Lady Thi Ne.

At the bottom of the chest sat a long, thin package wrapped in red silk. I opened it carefully. The contents resembled yellow-brown parchment or maybe a thin piece of tanned leather. Stretched to a length of about twelve inches, the leather-like strip had the drawing of a long dragon from head to tail in dark blue ink. A dragon tattoo. I then realized this would be my only meeting with the Lady's rival, Cheng Shih.

As I made my way back to the Perfume River to hitch a sampan ride to Hue City, I started counting up the days in my head. Too many had passed. By now the *S.S. Pedang* had sailed without benefit of a First Mate, and I was stranded like the captain had warned. But my family obligation was fulfilled and I now had the financial resources to look over the city and possibly explore some of the twists and turns of the Song Huong River. Maybe enjoy the perfume of the flowers this trip. Or even take one of those tourist excursions to some of the Royal Tombs, see if there'd been any recent signs of digging. With a little luck, maybe I'd find that Lady again, only this time without her pistol in hand. She just might be worth the effort.

COAL BLACK HEART

As the coal train slowed for the station, Little Evo sat down at the open door of the boxcar. He dangled his legs out over the iron edged rim of the rough wood floor and made ready. His scuffed work boots swung free just a few feet above the trestle spanning Little Walnut Creek. Sluggish water in the creek below showed as black and desolate as the many slag heaps along the tracks just outside of town.

In his right hand, Evo clutched a small canvas bag containing everything he now owned. The end of his travel was almost in sight, and the way he saw it, the far end of the bridge seemed to be the best place to jump off the train. With heavy masses of evening clouds already turning the sky dark, he doubted that anyone else would be aware unless they were already looking for him here. Giving a strong push off the boxcar with his left hand, Little Evo hit the ground running.

The six o'clock train from the Chicago, Burlington and Quincy Railroad Company continued on. Brakes squealed against metal wheels as the engine rolled into the station on the town's third mail run of the day.

A short walk down the tracks, Little Evo approached the red-painted, two-story wooden depot and read the sign. *Brazil, Iowa. 256 miles west of St. Louis, 52 miles east of Van Wert, 95 miles to Keokuk.* Evo stared at the English words. What the sign didn't mention was how many thousands of miles he'd just traveled from the recently formed Kingdom of the Serbs, Croats and Slovenes to get to this middle land of America. By foot and train from Croatia to the port in Le Havre, France, then passage on a steamer across the Atlantic to Ellis Island, and finally hopping freight trains headed west to this small coal mining town in Iowa.

It had been a long trip, and at least twice he'd felt the paranoia of being pursued. The feeling started long before the lingering stare from a well-dressed man on a street corner in Vienna, and had continued with the brown-suited man that seemed out of place in one of the French villages along the route. Several times, Evo had changed his plans and direction of travel, but each change ate up time on the road. Now he hoped he'd arrived at his destination in time.

"I help you there, Mister?"

Evo turned to the voice. A stocky man with weathered skin and a brushy mustache faced him.

"I'm Kelly, the section boss for this railroad. I don't suspect you just dropped off one of our trains? Passengers are supposed to ride in the passenger cars. And they buy a ticket."

Evo shrugged off the accusation. "I'm looking for work."

"Try the coal mines." Kelly paused as if appraising him before continuing. "From the sound of your accent, you're one of them Croats. We got plenty of Croatians here, couple of them even run their own mines." Kelly pointed up the street at a building. "There's a party at the U.M.W.A. Hall tonight. Most everybody will be in attendance. Good place to ask around about a job."

Evo touched the brim of his cap in thanks and started off up the street. Half a block from the union hall, the commotion of individual band instruments warming up for the festivities floated out on the evening air. From the front windows of the building, pale yellow lights shined a welcoming beacon to Evo. The hubbub of voices in his native tongue gave warmth to his heart. A resting place at the end of a far journey. He stepped up on the porch and stood in the doorway.

At the back of the large room, band members sat up on a dais, tuning instruments and arranging sheets of music on wooden stands. Along the far side wall, several people sat at tables, conversing with other town folk. Close at hand, the near side wall contained tables laden with food. Evo inhaled the aroma of veal cutlets and saw the large platters of *gibanica*, a layered cheese pastry. His mouth grew moist with hunger.

Groups of men stood along the front wall, their talk animated with laughter, loud voices and hand gestures. One of these, an older man dressed in a white shirt and black suit coat and trousers detached himself from the nearest group and approached the doorway. The man's skin had the pallor of one who spent most of his days underground, white almost the color of milk. And when the fellow stuck out his gnarled muscular hand in welcome, Evo noticed the taint of black coal under the man's ragged fingernails.

"Mike Barach," said the old man in accent laden English. "You're new here, eh?"

"Ivan Ilijic. My friends call me Little Evo. Kelly, the

section foreman for the railroad, said this is where I should ask about work."

Mike grinned. "I can tell by the voice you're one of us, but I confess I'm not familiar with the surname. As I recall, most alliterative names like yours were handed out by monastery nuns to abandoned babies left at the orphanage. Oh..."

The older man scratched his head and started over. "So, no future for you in the old country and now you've emigrated to America. Good for you. Come on in, lad. No charge for you tonight."

Inside the union hall, Mike took Evo's canvas bag and stashed it in a storage closet near the front of the room. "Your belongings are safe here, we don't tolerate thieves. However, we do keep a bottle of *rakija*, brandy, on the shelf for them that don't carry their own flask in their pocket. Federal law these days prohibits liquor, but some of us make our own drink. Not a crime to our way of thinking."

Evo politely declined the offered bottle.

Mike poured him a generous swallow into a teacup anyway.

"Go ahead, lad, you won't be used to the water here. The *rakija* kills the organisms. At least that's what I tell my old woman."

With a grin, Evo took the cup. "In that case." He threw back his head and downed the brandy.

"Good, good," said Mike. "Now tell me about the old country. What's the news?"

Evo grew serious.

"Not so good. Despite objections from our people, the Serbs have put one of their own on the throne. It's now King Alexander the First of Serbia, and his people have passed a new constitution for the country. Our Croatian

Peasant Party boycotted the legislative assembly for several years, but it does not help our cause. The Serbs use their greater military power to enforce centralized rule from their capital of Belgrade. All taxes, military promotions, and banking policies are structured in favor of the Serbs and against us Croats."

"Ah," replied Mike, "It's good me and the old woman and kids emigrated several years ago, shortly after the Great War ended. My family now lives well here in America. No troubles, just work." Mike took a small flat glass bottle from his inside suit coat pocket and extracted the cork. "Here's to the old country." He tipped the bottle and swallowed.

"There's worse," muttered Evo. "The Serbs have plans to change the name of the country to Yugoslavia, and there are rumors that the King wishes to become an absolute ruler, a dictator. Our Croatian revolutionaries oppose the Serb and his policies."

Mike shook his head.

"It's enough that I fought on the losing side with them damn Austrians in the Great War. I'll donate some of my hard earned money to the Croatian cause to help the home folk, but there will be no more fighting for Mike Barach or any of mine."

Evo poured himself another short drink from the community bottle, but kept his next thoughts close to his vest. Mike's way of thinking was fine since the cause already had plenty of fighters. But for now, it was the Croatian money coming from America that the Serbs feared most. Large donations from the Fraternal Croatian Union of America helped finance the revolutionaries back home. The Serbs wanted to eliminate this source of funding.

With the back of his hand, Evo wiped brandy moisture

from his lips.

"Are there jobs to be had?"

Mike glanced around the union hall and pointed out a couple of men.

"That tall fellow over there is John Cvitonavich, he works at the Number 10 mine. And the stocky man at the next table is George Capan from the Peacock mine. You could've worked for 'Big Evo' Polich, but he died in a mine accident ten days ago. That's his widow Katerina in the corner."

Little Evo glanced at the round-faced, large-bosomed woman in the black dress and scarf. Even with the festivities going around her, she seemed to exist in a vacuum. So, the rumors were true. It had already started, and he had failed to protect the family.

"What kind of accident?"

"Big Evo was working in the partin, where the three sets of tracks used by small ponies to pull loaded cars up from a slope mine merge together as one track. A mule then pulls the car from the *partin* the rest of the way out to the surface. I heard that a connecting pin broke on one of the coal cars and it came roaring back down the track. Big Evo had his back turned and didn't get any warning before it smacked into him."

"Who had the mules in harness when the pin broke?" Mike frowned.

"Good question. Don't know as I ever heard."

"The widow still running the mine?"

"At two dollars a ton for pick work, Missus Polich's miners can't afford to be idle, so she's talking about opening up again in a few days. Go ask her."

"Thanks, I'll do that."

"You know," ventured Mike as he appeared to concentrate on the bottle in his hand, "it's almost weird with you two having the same first names. We lose 'Big Evo' down there in the hole and shortly afterwards a 'Little Evo' shows up top side to replace him."

"Ivan is a common name for us Croats."

Mike raised his head and took another swig of bootleg before popping the cork back into the bottle's mouth.

"That's true, that's true."

As he walked away, Evo considered the true nicknaming of both Ivan's. Not so weird if you knew the circumstances. His adoptive family already had an older son named Ivan, so when the nuns at the orphanage gave up little Ivan Ilijic to the Polich family, their older natural son became 'Big Evo' while the newly adopted orphan received the nickname of 'Little Evo.' But for reasons of safety lately, it had been better to travel with the old Ilijic surname which the nuns had recorded in the *Stanja Dus'a*, the church records. His journey to America had not been a time to leave an easy trail for the hunters to find.

Teacup of brandy in hand, Evo crossed the open dance floor and approached the widow in the corner. He doffed his cap.

"Missus Polich, I'm looking for work and I hear you may be opening your mine again."

When Katerina raised her head, Evo noticed the lifeless, despairing gaze in her wide brown eyes.

Then he lowered his voice to avoid the ears of bystanders.

"Your sorrow is my sorrow. In the old country, I was adopted into the Polich family. Big Evo was my adoptive brother."

He caught the faint glimmer of hope in Katerina's eyes.

"Can you prove it?" she whispered.

"I have no papers on me, except the ones the authorities gave me at Ellis Island, but I can tell you about the Polich family. Big Evo had two older brothers, both stayed in Croatia. Their parents could only afford for those two sons to marry and be supported by the family holdings. Thus, the third son, Big Evo, had two choices; he could make a *domazet* arrangement where he assumed the surname of his wife and then lived on her property, or he could emigrate to another country and start his own life. He wished to keep his family's name, so he chose to come to America where he met you and married here. I am his younger brother, Little Evo."

Katerina held his gaze as if carefully considering the next words she would speak.

"Shortly before he died, my husband received a letter from his family. The letter said men would come from the old lands and we should be careful. How do I know you are not one of these men?"

Evo considered her predicament, trust and fear being hard masters for anyone to be comfortable with, especially if they followed close on the heels of death.

"You are wise to be suspicious," he finally said. "But let me tell you everything that has happened, and then you can believe what you wish."

She said nothing, so he continued.

"Your father-in-law is now in hiding from the Serbian King's secret police, and both of your husband's older brothers have fled to the revolutionaries in the Dinaric Alps for safe haven. But, before they slipped away into the night, they sent two letters here to Big Evo. One letter warned of the situation with the King, and how the Serbs planned to stop the flow of money from émigrés to the revolutionaries. The second letter contained a document stolen from the King's minister. This document outlines the plans for King Alexander to take absolute control of the government. You've seen these two letters?"

Katerina nodded.

"My Ivan read me the contents of the first letter. But after he opened the second envelope, he became quiet and went off to smoke his pipe."

"What happened to the second envelope?"

"He placed it in his coat pocket and I never saw it again."

Evo glanced around the room to see if anyone were paying undue attention to them, then he pulled an empty wooden chair next to Katerina's and sat with his head close to hers.

"Big Evo's death was no accident. Besides being in possession of the stolen document, he collected money to be sent to the revolutionaries, and because of that you may be in danger yourself. The secret police may also suspect you have the missing document in your possession. They would do much to retrieve it."

"I don't know where it is."

"No matter. They won't believe you."

Katerina's head dropped.

"That explains why our house was entered on the day of Ivan's funeral while we were at the cemetery. I thought it was thieves and wondered why they hadn't taken anything. The silverware and my mother's broach were untouched, yet papers had been moved and furniture was out of place."

"Do you have any idea where your husband might have hidden anything of importance?"

She shook her head.

"The house and the coal mine are all we have. There has been no fresh digging in the yard or garden, so it's not buried outside. The business papers for the mine are kept in a metal box in the parlor, but I've been through them and the letters were not there." Katerina paused. "I think someone else has also looked through the box."

Evo leaned back in the chair to think. He watched as three men dressed in clean work clothes came in the front door of the union hall and headed in their direction. Time for private conversation was running out.

"Missus Polich," Evo said in a normal voice, "why not give me a job in your coal mine? And if you will rent me a room in your house, then I can help out with the chores until you can make other arrangements."

He watched as Katerina followed the movements of his eyes, and then as she turned to take in the approaching men. All three men removed their caps as they stopped in front of the widow. The man in the middle and slightly in front of the other two miners covered his mouth with a red patterned handkerchief as a wet cough escaped his lips.

Katerina Polich remained seated as she acknowledged the newcomers and made introductions.

"The man in front with the deep cough is Bill Edwards, my straw boss for the mine. The blond-haired youth on his right is Lars Greska, he's our driver. And the strong dark-haired gentleman to his left is Stepan Kruzich, one of the diggers."

Katerina motioned at Little Evo.

"This is Ivan Ilijic. I just hired him to work in the mine."

Lars and Stepan showed big grins.

"Then we'll be opening the slope again?" inquired Bill. "As the boss, the men wanted me to ask you, ma'am, about going back to work that is."

"We'll start in the morning, Mister Edwards. For now, I would appreciate it if you would take our new hire down to my house and tell my oldest son to put him up in the bedroom in the attic. On the way, be so kind as to fill

Mister Ilijic in on his duties so he's not totally ignorant when he starts work."

"Yes ma'am."

Evo said his thanks and farewell to the widow, then gathered up his canvas bag from the closet and followed Bill Edwards out into the night. During the one mile walk to Katerina Polich's house, Bill explained the workings of the Black Dollar Mine.

"We're a wagon mine."

"What's that?"

"You see, a railroad mine is located close enough to the tracks that they can load their coal directly onto the rail cars. We're a ways off, so we have to use a horse team and wagon to haul our coal to the railroad tipple. Costs us extra for a teamster. The Black Dollar is a small operation, but we got good ventilation. Not one of those dog holes with no air shafts to bring in fresh air from the top."

"What should I expect tomorrow?"

"I'll fix you up with some picks, a bar, a shovel, carbide lamp, white denim pants with double material in the knees and a lunch bucket. You'll gob out the bottom handle-deep with a pick, then use a long metal bar to drop the lower seam of soft coal onto the floor and shovel it into one of the coal cars. You pick out the clay that exists between the seams, then bar out the hard coal in the upper seam and shovel it. At quitting time, I'll make a chalk line on the floor and measure your progress. The rest, you'll learn as you go."

"As you say, I'll learn as I go. How safe is it down there?"

"The Black Dollar is luckier than some. Air's good, so we got no black damps, poisonous gases. All the shale and rock we dig out is used to form the road wall, which supports the roof. The other debris is used as backfill in areas we've already mined. Use your head and pay attention. Other than that, there's no guarantees."

As they approached the Polich house close to the mine, Evo had one last question.

"I heard the owner got killed by a runaway coal car in the *partin*. Was Lars driving the mule team?"

Bill stopped abruptly.

"What are you trying to say?"

Evo smiled in the moonlit darkness.

"I'm saying I don't want to have any accidents. Do I have to keep an eye on Lars?"

"Normally, Lars drives the pony teams inside the mine and he also drives the mule teams to pull the cars out of the *partin*. On that particular morning, he said the wagon teamster, Goran, was having trouble up top and asked for his help. Goran verifies his story. Guess only Big Evo knows who hitched up the mule team in the partin that day, and he's not alive to tell us who it was. Anything else on your mind?"

Evo shook his head.

"Fine then. I'll see you in the morning."

Bill stepped up on the porch and knocked on the door. When one of the Polich sons answered the knock, Bill made arrangements for Evo to stay, then left the porch without another word and took the path back toward town.

With the light from a kerosene lantern, Evo soon found himself in a small attic bedroom. A straight-back wood chair, a cherry wood commode with washing bowl and mirror, and a bed with a mattress filled the room. He reflected on how long it had been since he'd lain in a real bed. Weary from the long road, he fell quickly into a dreamless sleep.

Before the sun had risen, there came a soft knocking

on wood, the attic door swung open and a set of miner's clothes were placed on the floor just inside the room. The door shut again. Evo quickly dressed and went down to the kitchen where he received coffee, meat and bread for breakfast, and a lunch pail from Katerina. She said few words, mostly staring at him with her wide brown eyes, as if she were searching for answers to unspoken questions.

A short walk down the dirt path put him at the mine entrance. Bill Edwards met him in the entry and took him along the right side track down to the coal face. Several times, they walked stooped over to avoid bumping heads against the mine's ceiling.

"This is your place. It's about forty feet wide. And there's your starting chalk line. Lars will bring you a car to shovel into."

Bill gave him a handful of metal discs with the number seven stamped into the metal.

"Here's your work number. Every time you fill a coal car, hang your disc on a hook on the side of the car. I'll weigh the car top side on a balance beam and record the weight with your number. That's how we figure your tonnage. I'll be back in a couple of hours to check on you."

As Bill walked away, leaving him in semi-darkness, Evo heard the straw boss's deep wet coughing recede into the distance. Getting down on his knees, Evo proceeded to swing the pick horizontally into the clay and dirt beneath the bottom seam. In between swings, he caught the faint sound of regulated drops of water falling from the top chamber of the miner's lamp attached to the front of his cap. When the drops landed on the carbide chips in the bottom chamber of the lamp, the resulting hiss of gas provided flame and a reflected light by which to work in the hovering blackness.

Other water, regulated only by the laws of nature, dripped from the mine ceiling, landed with a muted splash on the dirt floor and trickled across into sumps to be pumped out later. Sounds echoed and faded away in the underground chambers. In the back of his mind, Evo wondered how long it would take for his own skin to turn pale without sunlight in this subterranean world. He was still on his knees digging when he heard the clacking of metal wheels on the nearby track.

"I brought you a coal car," shouted Lars. "Fill it up and I'll bring you another."

Evo grunted his thanks and continued digging. He'd shoveled out the bottom and started barring the lower seam of soft coal down to the floor when he again heard footsteps. The shuffling stopped far back in the shadows, out of the range of his carbide lamp. This voice had a heavy tinge of the Serb.

"We know who you are, Ivan. You came too late to warn your brother, but give us the document and we will leave you and the widow alone."

Evo raised the iron bar in front of his chest like a quarterstaff.

"Come out where we can talk like men."

"The document, Ivan, else the next funeral you attend will be the widow's."

"We don't know where any document is."

"Then find it. And when you do, hang a white towel on the front porch as a signal. We'll contact you."

Evo waited for more, but there was only silence, then a slight rustling noise farther up the tunnel. The man with the threats had slipped away. Evo took off running toward the space where he'd heard the voice, bounced off the road wall in the dark and sat down hard on the floor. Rising up again, he moved at a slower pace up the slope to the partin. No one there. Quickly, he ran up to the entry and outside.

Over by the loading chute, Bill stood giving last minute instructions to the teamster, Goran, who was about to take a wagon load of coal to the railroad tipple.

"Bill," shouted Evo, "did anyone just come out of the mine?"

"I didn't see anyone but you. Why?"

"Some man threatened me down near the track, then came top side."

Bill turned back to the teamster and asked if he'd seen anyone else come out of the entry. The teamster shook his head.

Evo quickly returned to the partin. Maybe the man had turned down one of the other two roadways. He was debating which set of tracks to follow when Lars came up the left track with two ponies hitched tandem to pull a loaded coal car.

"Lars, did anyone come down the roadway you're coming out of?"

"No."

Evo thought for a moment.

"Are there any Serbs that work down here in the Black Dollar?"

"Not down here."

"An outsider got into the mine then. I'll check down the middle track, see if I can find him."

As he followed the track down into the underworld chamber, Evo heard Lars shout something, but echoes bounced through the corridors and distorted the words. No matter, he'd talk with Lars later.

Down at the coal face, Evo heard miners at work on either side of him. He recognized the one on his right as Stepan Kruzich from the UMWA union hall.

"Stepan, did anyone pass by here in the last few minutes?"

The miner stopped shoveling and rested on the handle.

"The only one that's been close to my place was Lars when he brought me an empty car about a half hour ago and took my full one. Other than that, it's just been me here and Kennedy over there. You can ask him, but I'd a heard anyone coming down the middle track. Who you looking for?"

"I'm not sure."

Stepan grunted and went back to work.

Someone was lying, but Evo couldn't figure who. Bill Edwards, Lars Greska or Stepan Kruzich? None of them spoke with a Serbian accent, so where had the Serb come in? And how did the Serb know his true identity, since he'd told only the widow Katerina?

Returning to his place, Evo went back to picking, shoveling and loading. While he worked, he reflected on every conversation he'd heard and everything he'd seen since arriving in the town of Brazil. A piece was obviously missing, even though it might be in plain view. Or maybe there were several interrelated pieces he wasn't aware of yet. His adoptive mother had told him long ago there was a reason for everything, and a relationship for events that happened to any individual. It was up to Evo to find the reasons and the connection.

That evening, after supper, Evo started a search of the interior of the Polich house for any hiding place big enough to hold a paper document. On the first night, he and Katerina searched all the furniture for concealed compartments or recently repaired seams. On the second night, they tapped all the floors, walls and ceilings for hollow spaces. On the third, he checked under and around the heating stove, sink, cooking stove and cast iron bathtub.

He was ready to give up on the interior of the house, when on the fourth night, he began to remove the trim boards to check spaces between the walls and the floors and ceilings. Stepping up on the seat of a wooden kitchen chair, he grabbed the ornate trim board above the front room door. The board moved.

He glanced at the nails in the piece of trim. The heads had been cut off. Now with the heads missing, the two finishing nails operated only as guides to seat the trim board over the top of the door. As the board slid upward, it revealed an opening between the top of the doorframe and the wall. In the opening rested an envelope.

Checking to be sure no one else was in the room, Evo removed the envelope and opened it. Inside was the document stolen from the Serbian King's minister. The paper that Big Evo Polich had been killed for. Black anger and frustration flooded Evo's mind. Replacing the envelope in its hiding place, he slid the trim board back into position.

For two hours, Evo sat on the chair beneath the front doorway while he considered the problem and his options. He was vaguely aware of the widow entering the room, standing quietly for a while, then backing away and keeping her children from intruding on his solitude. In the early hours of morning he finally went upstairs to the attic and sought sleep.

For the next couple of days, he went to work in the Black Dollar Mine like all the other employees. With a sore back and blistered hands, he dug and barred and shoveled, all the while turning the events over in his mind. And he kept his ears tuned to any footsteps approaching in the dark. None came, except for Bill with his chalk line to check on progress, and Lars to bring empty coal cars and take away the full ones.

At the end of his shift, Evo trudged out of the mine and headed along the path to the Polich house. Up on the porch, he stopped. A white piece of paper, stuck into a crack in the door, fluttered in the light breeze. He smoothed the paper flat against the door and slowly read the hand printed words in large block letters.

> **ACCIDENT**
> **MEET ME AT UNION HALL**
> **K.**

Sudden fear seized his heart. Throwing open the front door, Evo hollered for the Polich children. Silence came back from every corner. He wondered briefly if there had been a cave-in at one of the other mines, but then Katerina wouldn't have taken the children. No, one of the kids must've been hurt. He only hoped it had nothing to do with problems from the old country.

Leaving the front door wide open, he raced toward town. In less than eight minutes, he'd covered the one mile distance to the railroad tracks near the depot. As he crossed the tracks and headed past the railway station, he heard Katerina's voice ahead. She was just leaving the general store. Each of her children following close behind carried a box or a bag from the store. She stopped short at seeing him and smiled.

"Evo, where are you going so fast?"

He slowed to a walk.

"You said for me to meet you at the union hall."

"Not I. Where did you get that notion?"

"The note you left on the door."

"What note?"

Evo didn't wait to hear the rest of her questions. He turned back the way he'd come and ran even harder. His mind thought furiously. A quarter of an hour round trip. That was enough time for anything to happen. Lungs burning, he topped the hill and started down toward the house.

As the front of the Polich residence came in sight, he saw a man come out of the doorway and onto the porch. Evo slowed down when he recognized the man as Bill Edwards. Bill must've come by to check on things. Dropping to a fast walk to catch his breath, he watched in disbelief as Bill splashed liquid from a round can onto the wood porch, and tossed the can through the doorway into the interior. The straw boss then struck a match, touched it to a torch in his hand and applied flame to the drenched wood. Fire quickly grew along the front of the house.

At Evo's shout, Bill turned, then threw the torch inside and took off running on the path to the mine. Gasping for breath, Evo followed.

Near the entry to the Black Dollar, a spasm of coughing shook Bill's body. His pace decreased to a lurching walk. Straight ahead lay open pasture and gentle hills. To the right gaped the mine entrance. Bill turned into the darkness of the mine and disappeared.

Evo paused at the entry. When his breathing returned to normal, he descended to the *partin*. Extra mining equipment sat against the road wall. Sliding a carbide lantern onto the metal frame attached to his cap, Evo left it unlit, but grabbed up an iron bar for a weapon. Slowly he moved into the encompassing dark, homing in on the occasional wet coughing sounds emanating from deep in the cavern, down along the right side track. Twice he adjusted course to allow for the confusing echoes, but always he moved closer. Then silence.

Evo crouched, listening. Nothing. Bill had seemed to be headed toward the place where Evo had spent the last week picking and shoveling. Cautiously, Evo continued, feeling his way along the track. Arriving at the coal face, he abandoned the track and felt his way with one hand on the wall. He stopped. Nothing.

Taking one more step, he heard the rasp of a choked back cough and ducked. A shovel sliced the air over his head and banged against the coal face. Quickly, he swung the iron pry bar upward and heard a broken grunt. A stumbling noise came to his ears, then a dragging sound as if a great effort were being made to move an object. The noise retreated. The dragging ceased and heavy breathing took over.

Evo adjusted the water regulator in the top chamber of his carbide lantern. When the gas began to hiss, he spun the flint for a spark. Light erupted from the lantern and he moved forward. Eventually, the yellow light shone on Bill curled up in the gobbed out bottom, seeking concealment in the hollow beneath the lower seam of soft coal. Bill held his arms across his ribs and seemed to be having trouble breathing. Evo squatted down a short distance away.

"You up to talking, Bill?"

"Not really. I got this bad pain in my side right now."

"You burned the house, Bill. What were you thinking?"

"Ah, Evo, it were nothing personal with you. It's just that when we didn't hear from you and Katerina, the Serb figured you'd found the document and meant to use it. So he had me write that note on the door to get you out of the way while I set the fire. He couldn't take a chance on the document getting out."

Bill coughed and groaned.

"I'm in pain here, boy. Get me a doctor."

"If it's any comfort to you," replied Evo, "the document probably burned up in the fire. Now, who's the

Serb?"

"Goran, the teamster that hauls our coal to the railroad. He never spoke in front of you because he feared you would recognize the accent. But you'll never catch him now. Once he knows how bad this got botched up, he'll be gone and someone else will come in. An unknown."

"How did he know I was here?"

"The secret police in your country got to the serving girl in your eldest brother's house. They had something on her family, so she told the police everything she heard in the house. Your trip was no secret and he had your description."

Another spasm of coughing shook Bill's body. Evo noticed a trickle of blood at the corner of the man's mouth.

"I think you're dying, Bill, best tell me everything."

"Get me a doctor and I'll tell you whatever you want to know."

"First things first, Bill. Why you?"

"Can't you hear the cough? I've got the black lung from years in the mines. I need money to go somewhere warm and dry away from all this coal dust, but I'm never gonna make that kind of cash down here in the dark. The Serb paid me well for what I did."

"And what you did was kill my brother, Big Evo, with a coal car."

"Ah now, that was purely an accident. Sure, I was driving the mules, but the connecting pin must've been weak. I didn't bother to tell the Serb that though, I just took his money and let him think otherwise.

Bill clutched his ribs as he coughed until the problem subsided.

"Where's that doctor you promised? Get him and I'll give you all the money Old Goran paid me for doing nothing."

Evo rose into a half crouch. Cold anger froze his heart. "You're lying, Bill, telling only partial truths. And I'll take no money stained with my brother's blood. But don't worry about that cough any more. It won't be bothering you much longer."

Sticking his iron bar into the clay above the lower coal seam, Evo pried down. The seam fell. He inserted and pried, inserted and pried, until the clay was gone and the upper seam of hard coal had also fallen. Then he attacked the rocks in the mine ceiling, banging and screaming. At last, the rage wore down. He stood silent, surprised at the amount of violence in his soul, yet not repentant enough to make the sign of the cross at the death of another human being.

"It's a coal black heart you have," came the voice from behind. "We'll have to change your name to Black Evo. Can't say I blame you though. If he had murdered my brother, I'd a probably done the same."

Evo whirled to find Stepan standing in the background.

"Don't worry about me," said Stepan. "Big Evo and me was friends. And after what I just heard, Bill only got what he deserved. I'll say nothing."

Evo hesitated.

"You can live with this?"

Stepan shrugged.

"I hear the good coal is thinning out in this section anyway, so you might want to wall off this part of the face and pile on lots of heavy stones, make a solid road wall, floor to ceiling. To my way of thinking, it wouldn't do to have Old Bill's spirit walking around down here in the dark while I'm digging."

"You want me to put up a solid wall?"

"I do. Us miners can be a superstitious lot. As hard as

I work, I don't dream much at night, but if I get to hearing strange noises behind me down in the Black Dollar, then I'll be moving on. Till then, you got a miner."

Evo nodded. Then needing the sudden purity of fresh air, he made his way top side. Sunlight faded in the west as he walked out of the entry. Soon the darkness of night would envelope him and his thoughts. Not as dark as the black hole in the bottom of the mine, nor of the emotions warring in his heart, but darkness just the same. Having started life abandoned by nameless parents, he now found himself in the land of opportunity where he had failed to save a brother, an important member of the caring family that had taken him in from the orphanage.

Perhaps Stepan had been right in what he said down in the mine. Black Evo was the appropriate name for him. The only hope he felt for his own redemption now was to somehow protect what little family he still had left.

DEARLY DEPARTED

"Gentlemen, gentlemen," Jock rapped the iron tipped base of his walking stick on the stone floor, "listen close. I have dire news which may concern the welfare of us all."

"Gentlemens he calls us," mocked a raspy voice from the other side of the torch-lit vaults, "and us with scarce two farthings to clink together in our pockets."

"Aye, McPhee, you said it a-right," cried a third man, "surely we'd all be honest folk making a tidy profit up in the open sunlight if'n it weren't for the Excise Tax."

Raw laughter burst from the rag-tag group assembled under one of the enclosed stone arches beneath Southgate Bridge in the heart of Edinburgh.

"Quiet," roared Jock, "this has naught to do with Old English Georgie laying a whiskey tax on Mother Scotland to pay for his war against Napoleon and the Frenchies."

"Then what did you gather us here for?" McPhee rasped.

Jock raised his arms spread wide until the murmuring died out.

"Three of our brethren under the bridge have gone missing in the last several days."

Cries of "Who?" rang out from the mob.

"Old Liam and Young Patrick," replied Jock, "both of them fellow stillers from here in the vaults under South Bridge, and..."

"Maybe the Excise Man got them," interrupted McPhee. "So who's the third?"

"...Black Murphy from a vault on the other side of Cowgate."

"You be speaking of everyone's friend Murph, sole proprietor of the Gilded Swan? Murph who runs a brothel, not a whiskey still? What's that got to do with us?"

"My point exactly. Something new has come down into our world."

"Ah, one of Murph's gilded swans probably knifed him in a drunken brawl over a few coins, that's all."

"Listen to me carefully," implored Jock. "It's sure we have our usual killings from whiskey fights and thieves' feuds, however them bodies is always found soon enough. But, our three mates have completely disappeared. No trace left behind. If'n the Excise Men had gotten Liam and Patrick, then they'd also have seized all their equipment. There's been no raids lately, and their stills remain here in the vaults right where their owners left them in operation for a short time to take care of other business..." He paused for effect. "...and then those two fine gentlemen never came back. No blood, no signs of a struggle in their places. Nothing was disturbed, and I'm sure you know how valuable the copper tubing on a still is."

Calls of "aye, we'll give you that," and a shout of, "so it wasn't for theft," burst from the dark assemblage.

"And the Excise Man would have no interest in Black

Murph," rasped McPhee in his gravel voice, "cuz as far as I know, even Royal Georgie the Fourth hasn't put a tax on those particular services." He grinned in the torchlight.

Scattered chuckles of amusement rose from the crowd.

"So what are you saying, mon?"

Jock softened the timbre of his voice. "I'm saying be careful when you go about your business down here in the black tunnels. Keep your eyes and ears open when you pass in and out through the stone tenements enclosing both sides of South Bridge. And, if you do find anything not ringing true, then send me one of the tunnel rats with a message right away. That's all I'm saying."

Mutters of assent rolled forward from the assembled men as they gradually drew into small groups and drifted away in various directions. Long shadows jerked and crept along the walls as the departing men carried their lanterns and torches down the distant passageways. Silence soon filled the arched vault.

Now that the mob had left, McPhee sidled up to the front of the cool dim room. "What do you think it is, Jock, that's come amongst us?" he asked quietly.

"Don't know, but it has an oppressive feel to it, like death has taken on a new form under the arches. Sometimes when I cease my labors and the vaults grow still, only the water dripping down from the roof, I feels a chill on the back of my neck, like the Grim Reaper himself is exhaling right behind me. Damned if I don't."

Jock buttoned his coat higher around his neck and took a quick glance over his shoulder.

"Maybe ye better go see if young Douglas has returned. He's been gone a long while, and I need a word with him."

Douglas

"Can't say, Mister, as if I've seen you any time before

down here in the dark."

"Can't say I've seen you either, me boyo."

"Then it's time we met. Me name's Douglas and I sees pretty much everything what goes on under the bridge. That's cuz I'm one of the tunnel rats."

"Tunnel rats, you say?"

"Aye, all us rats are orphans what run errands for the stillers and the brothels. Earns our daily bread for us, you see."

Douglas scratched his stomach before continuing.

"You must be one o' them newcomers who has found their way into the vaults. We gets lots of 'em lately. Some stay cuz they got no other home to go to. Others set up shop as stillers or work the brothels, and we've got several dens of thieves. I'd watch out for those lean gentlemen if I was you."

Raising his Bulls-eye lantern a bit higher, Douglas took a better look at the man standing before him.

"They'd cut your throat for a good coat, though I can't say yours is very fancy. The elbows look worn out like you was a common laborer, one of them Irish fellows maybe come in to work on the Union Canal a few years back, eh? Hard work and low pay is what I heard whenever I was topside. So what's your game?"

"Ah, begging your pardon, me boyo, but what says to you I'm a newcomer?"

"That's easy, Mister, your lantern's all burned out and you got no torch to find your way. There's over a hundred vaults enclosed by stone in this place. A man could wander down here for a long time... if you wasn't smart enough to keep a good light with you, that is."

"Tell me more then, boy. You seem to know it all."

"About this place? Well, they constructed it before I was born. Me Da worked on it. When I was a wee lad and he was still alive, he told me once that the bridge was never built to go over water. Appears the land about was too hilly and rocky for carts and people, so they made a bridge straight up to the ridge spine so as the road on top connects right into High Street. You know, part of the Royal Mile, that road what runs all the way from the Castle up on the hill down to the Palace at Holyrood below? Yeah, well, the bridge gave people somewhat of a smooth road to travel on to get up to High Street. There's nineteen arches in all beneath South Bridge, but only one arch has a street through it. That's Cowgate, the other eighteen got stone tenements built right up against 'em. When they was first built, the enclosed arches got used as free storage by businesses in those stone buildings."

"Shops don't use them any more?"

"Nah, somebody forgot to seal the bridge road, so when the rains came, water dripped down into the vaults below, ruined whatever goods got stored there. Pretty soon, the shops moved out and the homeless moved in. That you, one of them without a home?"

"Let's just say I'm looking around, me boyo."

"That's what they all say at first, Mister. Well then, just follow the light from my Bulls-eye lantern and watch your step."

Douglas swung the lantern in a wide arc to show the passage. Long shadows danced behind piles of debris on the floor.

"There's some real live rats infesting the damp corners of this place. Them big fellows are so ferocious that cats don't bother to come down here anymore. Mostly the rats will leave you alone if you gots a lit torch or a bright lantern, but I wouldn't want to be all by myself here in the dark. It's blacker than the Devil's heart. Tell you what, I'll take you as far as a door back into one of these stone tenements, then you're on your own from there. You might not want to come back, lessen you got a good torch or some kind of light to see by."

Angus

At the sound of leather scuffing on wood, Angus peered back over his shoulder.

"Oh, hullo there, didn't hear you come in while I was working, but I thinks you've made a wrong turn somewheres, Mister. This is my room, my sons and I pays the rent on it in this tenement building. So what do you want here?"

"Sorry, I must've lost my way in the dark hallway."

"You're not the Excise Man, are ye?"

"No, no."

"Guess I could've seen that for myself. Your coat and trousers look a little threadbare for one of them devils. Of course, from your accent, I'd take you for Irish. And from the calluses on your hands, I'd say you're common labor. Am I right?"

"You're a very observant man, me boyo."

"That I am, and from my observations I take you to be one of the homeless men roaming around South Bridge, eh? So move along, I've got no room for you here. 'Sides, I've got business to do. Seems everybody's in a hurry for their goods these days."

Angus made a shooing motion with the back of his hand, but the intruder seemed to be in no hurry to leave.

"My heartiest apologies," said the newcomer. "I meant no harm." His hand moved to his coat pocket. "Tell you what, friend, as a matter of good intentions on my part, let me offer a dram of whiskey to share with you. Consider it penance for my untimely intrusion."

"Whiskey, eh?" Angus cleaned his palms on the legs of

his trousers. "Let me see it then." He held the small bottle up to the light. "Could be the color and clarity look right. I'll tell soon enough about the flavor."

Liquid gurgled in the candle lit room as Angus tipped the glass bottle.

"Ah, it's smooth on the tongue like some of Old Liam's whiskey. If you got this from him, then you're a righteous man. I'll have me another swallow if you don't mind."

"Please do, and perhaps I can be of some help with your business here, whatever it is?"

"I sees you looking at the hole in my tenement wall and the tail of the rope hanging out near my other hand. You must be some curious, eh?"

"Aye, that's true enough, and admittedly its very strangeness begs for someone to ask questions about that hole. Now if the hole was in the floor, then I'd say maybe you had your own deep well. But there it is, a hole in the wall." The newcomer shrugged. "Of course it's none of my concern."

"No, it's not your concern, laddie. But lucky for you, I'm a good judge of men, and you look to be friendly enough, sharing your whiskey with me and all, so I'll tell you this much. I'm a *dropper*."

"A *dropper*?"

"Aye. The stillers below need to get their loads of sugar and malt, yeast, coal and peat without being followed by the Excise Man back to their stills, so I cut a hole in my tenement wall which leads down through the roof of the stone arches and into the vaults. Then I use a bucket on a rope to drop their supplies down to 'em. They pays me in money or whiskey. All the same to me. I'd give you a job, but I have no need of help."

"You must get lonely here by yourself."

"Nah, it's not like down there in the darkness of the

vaults without a drop of sunshine. With me being up here in the outside world, I goes out and hears things. If the Excise Man makes a raid somewheres, I hears about it and passes word down below."

"An interesting life you lead."

"It is, it is, but that's not all, laddie. Here, give me another swallow. Ah, good stuff. Now where was I?"

"I believe you were speaking of the outside world and what you hear."

"Ah yes, I hears all the gossip topside, everything what's going on. Maybe you know that university close by? Well, for one thing you'd be surprised to hear what them students of the old Barbers and Surgeons Guild are up to these days. Many's the rumors of wild depravity and corruption in that place of learning. With what them students is doing, I can tell you, I wouldn't want to be caught dead in their so called school. Learning? Hah." Angus wiped his mouth on the cuff of his left sleeve before handing back the half empty bottle. "And as for me being lonely, my two sons should be back shortly with another load of supplies."

"Perhaps I should be on my way then. Good day to you."

"Good day to you too, friend, but keep in mind, it's probably best if you don't come back this way, a dram of sociable whiskey or no. My sons, not knowing you to be a generous man with your liquid possessions, might up and take you the wrong way."

Old Donald

"Och, sorry there, sir, didn't mean to startle like that, but I didn't see you standing so close in the darkness. Your lantern must've gone out, eh? Well that's all right, sir, you can walk with Old Donald here and I'll show you a lighted way through these dark caverns."

"That's kind of you, me boyo."

"Not a problem. I'm down here in the vaults looking for my younger brother anyway. He seems to have disappeared. His name's Patrick. Don't suppose you've seen him?"

"No, can't say as I have, but then this is my first time in the vaults."

"I was thinking I hadn't seen you down here before, but then as I recall from being topside now and again, you run a lodging house not too far from the university where all them students are."

"Uh, yes, the missus and I do keep a place for lodgers."

"That's right, I'd heard something about her first husband passing on from the fever or some kind of blood ailment a couple years back. His name was Logue or Log or something like that. Lucky for his widow you took up with her in her time of bereavement. I says these days a woman needs a man to help look after a place like that. You never know who you might get for lodgers, some of 'em can be mighty rough people. Not everybody's honest folk like you and me."

"Generous of you to say so, ...Donald."

"I notice you wrinkling your nose somewhat. Don't worry about it, sir, that's why people calls this city *Auld Reekie*. You'll get used to the smell down here if you stays long enough. Mostly it comes from the lingering dampness, peat smoke and all the rotting garbage what folks throw away into the odd corner here and there. But then I'm lucky in that regard cuz the odors don't bother me none. Guess my nose got burned out from working my still all these years and breathing in the fumes. Of course, the grain dust makes me sneeze a lot, other than that it's no bother."

Donald walked carefully forward with his Bulls-eye lantern opened wide to spread light on the littered floor in the passageway. Here, side walls sparkled from clinging moisture making its way downward, while soot blackened stones loomed overhead, gradually receding into an arched ceiling which disappeared into the upper blackness. Drips of water gave a hollow echo.

"Watch your step there, sir."

"Evidently you've been down here a while then, Donald?"

"Aye, my brother and I both. We make our whiskey in separate places, but Young Patrick don't come over much lately cuz he says my vault in the upper arch has acquired the whiff of a dead cow to it. Me, I don't smell anything in the air. Maybe there's some bad vapors coming up from the vault below me, but I've never taken a look to see what's down there. Some denizens of these rooms, you understand, don't appreciate unexpected company."

"I'll keep that in mind, Donald."

The old man held his Bulls-eye lantern out to one side.

"Here, sir, come on up in the light beside me. If you keep lagging back behind me like that, you'll trip over something on the stone floor and injure yourself. That wouldn't do at all. I'd have to leave you and go for help. It wouldn't be pleasant for you, you keeping company with the rats down here. And who knows what kind of rough people might find you lying helpless all alone in the dark. No sir, I couldn't have that on my conscience. It's bad enough me own brother has seen fit to disappear for several days and me looking all over for him in case he's lost and hurt somewhere. No, no, sir, I insist, come on up here and walk beside me in the lantern light. It's much safer for you."

Fergus

"Ah, Mister Hare, it's a bright sunny day out here under the autumn sky, but you're looking a little pale and under the weather. What you need is a drop or two of good whiskey. Come on into my tavern and I'll stand you to a glass. I've been having one of them bad days myself and could use the company if you don't mind listening. We can sit on this bench in the corner with none to bother us. There you go, now have a taste with me, perhaps this'll cheer us both up. You can tell me your problems and then I'll go on about mine own."

"There's not much I can tell..."

"From the look of you, I'd say it's money what's worrying your head."

"You could say that, me boyo, and I wouldn't argue."

"Let me assure you, Mister Hare, that no man ever has enough. No matter what he does to get it, the coins seem to slip right through his fingers. But then I'd have thought your missus' lodging house would provide well for the two of you."

"As you say, me boyo, it's never enough."

"Then a man must seek other means of income on the side."

"That I have."

"That's well for you then, you've naught to worry about." Fergus passed his open hand across his chin, his brow furrowing into a deep crease. "As for me and mine, a dear old friend seems to have disappeared off the very face of the earth. It's Mary Haldane what's missing." Fergus shook his head sadly. "She's a regular character here in the neighborhood. I may have spoken of her before in one of our conversations."

"Not that I recall."

"Ah, well, admittedly she's a local prostitute for many years, and yet a kindly soul to all who know her. And, in truth it's her fine looking daughter Peggy I'm interested in." Fergus took a deep draught from his cup, then set it gently down beside him on the bench before continuing. "Mary and I had a nice talk here in the tavern a few days ago and she was to drop in and see me again afterward on her way home. I've seen naught hide nor hair of her since. It's a mystery to me is what it is."

"Perhaps she forgot as older folk are wont to do and merely continued on her journey home."

"I wondered that myself, Mister Hare, and seeing as to how she has been a mite forgetful in her waning years, I sent a boy around to her lodgings. The room was all closed up and her neighbors haven't seen anything of her for a few days. Peggy's been searching for her mother everywhere since then, and now Peggy has also disappeared. I fear the worst, robbers and murderers."

"Not to worry, Fergus, your friend and her daughter will probably turn up in a day or two. Here, let's drink to their good health and safe return."

Fergus raised his glass to clink with his drinking companion.

"You have some rough edges about you, Mister Hare, but you've a soft heart and a kind manner. No doubt that has something to do with your financial problems?"

"No doubt it does, Fergus, no doubt. My apologies now, but I must be on my way. Business, you understand?"

"Aye, the worry of earning enough money to keep one's body and soul together. Go on then and good luck to you."

"Thank you, me boyo, I may need the luck."

Wee Arthur

"Calm yourself, Wee Arthur, and tell me what's worrying you."

"It's like this, Master Jock, Douglas sent me topside to find Daft Jamie. Jamie always has some treats for us orphans and he teaches us new games to play, if'n we happens to have a little free time that is. So I went looking for him in some of the closes near the Bridge. But I dinna find him there, so I came back into the vaults."

"Go on."

"I was late to meet up with Douglas, you see, so I was taking what I thought was a short cut through a part of the lower vaults I hadn't been in for a long time. And, as I was running down some steps, I slipped on the wet stone and banged my elbow. The fall put out my lantern and I had no way to relight it."

"In this place, Wee Arthur, one should always carry extra matches on his person."

"I did that, sir, but my matches must've gotten soft from being in all the damp down here."

Jock patted the boy on the shoulder to comfort him.

"What happened to worry you so without a light?"

"Like I said, Master Jock, I was in a lower part of the arches I hadn't been in for a long while. And since I couldn't see in that great darkness, I had to put my hands in front of my face and feel my way."

"Aye, that must have given a fright to a young lad your age."

"Oh, sir, you don't know the half. The place had the faint smell of a dead cow, and the farther I moved into the vault the stronger the odor grew."

"There's much garbage down here, lad."

"Yes sir, but then I touched it with my finger tips."

"Touched what?"

"The shoe."

"There's lots of cast off old shoes in these tunnels, boy."

"Aye, but this one had a foot in it."

"A drunk sleeping it off most likely."

"No sir, this man was cold as the stone floor. I felt his throat and face for warmth, but his soul had long departed."

"Show me where the body lays, Wee Arthur, and we'll soon see who it is."

"I know who it is, sir."

"Who?"

"Daft Jamie, the one I went to find. I knew him by the feel of his snuff box and spoon in his vest pocket. His snuff spoon had seven holes in it so as Jamie could tell what day of the week it was." Wee Arthur took a moment to run the length of his coat sleeve along under his nose, and sniffed. "But the body's no longer there, sir."

"What? Why not?"

"See, I'd found my way out of that cold vault and was feeling my way along a damp wall when I heard shuffling noises and voices back in the vault I'd just left behind me. I was about to cry out and ask for help, but by the way those two men were talking, they already knew the dead body was there. They were the ones hiding it in the vault until nightfall when it was safe for them to come and carry it out concealed inside a tea chest."

"Did you recognize either of the men?"

"No sir, just that they had Irish accents, but there was some talk about the dead man being worth ten pounds."

"Ten pounds? Daft Jamie never had that much money in his life. Are you sure of what they said?"

"Oh, yes sir, they said they would get ten pounds from

a man named Knox. They only hoped this Knox would be in when they came calling in the dead of night."

"I know of no one named Knox here under the arches, nor in the stone tenements around us. Well, I'll look into it and see what I can find. Now go about your duties, Wee Arthur. Have you seen young Douglas? I have need of him."

"No, Master Jock, I've not laid eyes on Douglas since he sent me topside. He was going to run an errand while I was gone, but I have no knowledge of where he went."

"I see. Well, if you find him, send him straight to me. We have an urgent matter before us."

#

Once again, Jock rapped his iron tipped stave upon the stone floor of the torch lit vault under South Bridge.

"It's been some several weeks since last we gathered, Gentlemen, but I now have grave news to impart."

The crowd of men stirred, then settled.

"Give it up, Jock," one called out. "We haven't all day."

Jock removed his hat and held it before his chest.

"It appears we've lost one of our tunnel rats. Our boy Douglas has disappeared same as our other three friends did, and whereas we've not found the young lad's body, I fear we now know where he's gone."

"Speak out, Jock, tell us what you know."

"Angus, our dropper, sent word down from the topside. He says the police made an arrest a few days ago. It would appear that the Resurrectionists have been operating in our very vaults under South Bridge."

"Grave robbers? We've no cemeteries down here, and there's been no funerals topside for Liam or Patrick."

"Aye, and none for Murph or Young Douglas either. But these two Resurrectionists have put a new twist on the game."

"How's that, Jock?"

"They're a pair of topsiders, those two Bills named Burke and Hare. Seems they got tired of waiting for people to die so as they could go dig them up from the cemetery in the dead of night. Instead, they found it easier to create their own corpses direct from live folk. And, if'n the bodies were still fresh, then those two got paid a higher price from Doctor Knox over at the medical university. This good doctor used our friends in his anatomy class."

"The police has caught these murderers then?"

"Aye, they was hiding the corpse of their last victim, an old lady named Mary Docherty, under the bed, but some of the lodgers seen the body and went to the law. Poor woman was later found on a dissection table in Doctor Knox's classroom and was identified by a friend of hers. Now, the Lord Advocate, Sir William Rae, has offered Hare full immunity from prosecution if he confesses and testifies against Billy Burke. It'll be the gallows for that one."

"Rightly so."

"It's a shame. The vaults won't be the same without Liam and Patrick."

"And Young Douglas."

"Bless them all."

Jock lifted his flask of whiskey to the assembled men.

"To our dearly departed, may they rest in peace."

"Aye," rumbled McPhee, "and may Burke and Hare soon face them all on the other side."

SNITCH

"**H**ey, hey, Bud, get off your high horse. I'm just trying to survive on these streets. If you ain't been here, you don't know what it's like. Yeah, yeah, I know, 'snitch' has got a bad connotation to it. Personally, I like the term 'cooperating individual' better. These days, MTV's got all them rappers preaching in their music about how wrong it is to snitch off a criminal when he pops a cap on some dude he don't like. But, them rappers, they're all making big bucks playing at being gangsters, so what do you expect them to say? It's all a game to them. Meantime, the real gangsters, their hard crime is what puts them in jail doing hard time, if'n they even get caught that is. Now you, you're just a citizen, I can tell you ain't involved in this street thing, but I tell you what, you want crime out of your neighborhood, then you best be thanking a snitch for doing his job. And it's a dangerous one at that. Let me tell you my story while we're having a drink here, and then you make up your own mind about this snitch thing before you be calling me names."

\#

Mostly, I try to stay out of the spotlight. Don't do your career any good to have the cops breathing down your neck. That's why I usually front somebody else off to do the exposure work. Like, I don't do pharmacy burglaries myself. Nope, what I do is when some amateur rips off a pharmacy, he knows he can bring the drugs to me and I'll identify them for him. That way he knows what he's selling on the streets and how much he can get for it. Half the young guys these days can't tell an upper from a downer by reading the name on the label. Naturally, I take a ten percent cut of the merchandise for my services. After that, my ol' lady sells our share to whoever she knows. Even then, you gotta be careful, but it pays the rent.

Anyway, two weeks go by after one of them deals so I'm off hanging with some friends and I get a phone call on the cell from my ol' lady Patricia. She'd been bagged. I told her and I told her, only sell to those you know. Well, somebody she's been doing business with for years brought in somebody new and swore they were first cousins or something. Yeah, like I was born yesterday. Turns out this alleged first cousin that Patricia sold to was a narc. Now she needs bail and what's she gonna do, she can't do time.

I know she's got a habit, and if the cops sweat her long enough, she'd give up her own mother. So, I go on down to the jail to see what's what. Just as soon as I start asking questions at the desk, I know I'm in trouble.

"Felix," says a man in suit and tie as he steps up beside me and grasps my arm at the elbow, "I think you better come on in to my office."

"Who the heck are you?" I ask, but I've already got a

fair idea because he's steering me toward the elevator and I know the Vice Squad has offices up on the third floor.

"Detective Morales," he replies.

"You got some ID?" Not that it makes much difference at this point, but I like to know who I'm talking to.

With his free hand he extracts a leather case from his suit coat inside pocket and flips it open. The gold shield in the case says Detective and has a number on it. Damn.

"Where we going?" I ask, but I'm not feeling real polite at this point.

"Upstairs where you and I can talk in private."

That's a relief of sorts, cuz if Patricia had totally given me up to save herself, I'd probably be on my way direct to a holding cell. Hell, life is cruel.

Next thing I know, I'm standing in a small room looking at a solitary table and two chairs, one chair on either side of the table. There's a large mirror on the back wall, but everybody, even civilians, know it's only a mirror from one side and that there's probably somebody standing on the other side of the glass watching what's going on in this room like they had their own private window. Me, I'm not saying a word, I'm just waiting to hear what this guy has on his mind. Never give up nothing you don't have to, cuz it might be something the cops don't know about.

Detective Morales leaves me alone in the room for several minutes, then comes back with *one* cup of coffee. Don't even ask me if I want any. Then he takes his time removing his suit coat, arranging it neatly on the back of his chair before sitting down. Me, I'm still standing, not committing to nothing, waiting to see what's up here. It don't bother Morales, he just spends several minutes flipping through pages in a manila folder. It's so quiet I can hear the chair squeak when he shifts his weight.

At the top of one page, I can see an old mug shot of me when I was younger and did something stupid. It was a first offense deal, so I got off light with straight probation. Did two years of trying to look like a good civilian, then the probation officers got busy with real criminals and didn't have time for me no more. So now me in the mug shot is staring at me standing up. One of us is upside down here.

Detective Morales turns to a yellow legal pad covered with lots of hand-written notes in black ink. He studies them in silence, not saying a word to me yet, but now I know the cops are going to make me an offer I can't refuse. Finally, he turns to an empty page in the legal pad and picks up a ballpoint pen. He looks up at me and I see it coming.

"It's like this, Felix. We arrested Patricia for the distribution of controlled substances."

Translated, this means she got stupid, sold some of our stolen pharmacy pills to a sneaky narc and now she's sweating in a holding cell upstairs wondering what's next and how bad will the withdrawals be if she don't get back to our hidden stash pretty soon. So yeah, I'm fairly sure she gave me up for something I did in the past, else they wouldn't be talking to me. I just don't know how much she gave them.

"What does Patricia getting busted have to do with me?"

Detective Morales would make a good poker player, his face don't give nothing away. And, he's got them cop eyes that look straight inside you like he knows everything you're thinking. You got no secrets with this guy.

"You're a bright boy, Felix, so here's the deal. You sign up to become a cooperating individual for us, and then you get to go free this time."

"I walk?"

"Yeah, *this* time you walk."

"What about Patricia?"

"It's her first offense, we'll make sure she gets probation."

Now I know that on a first offense, she'll probably get probation anyway, or at most a light sentence and be back on the streets in a few months. But I also know that if I don't take this offer from Morales right now, then one of them other detectives is gonna catch Patricia when her withdrawals is working on her like sharp fingernails in her guts, and then she's gonna cough up everything she knows about me. I gotta take the deal and get her out of here quick.

"Throw in a PR bond so Patricia gets out tonight?"

Detective Morales hesitates just long enough to let me think maybe I'm driving a hard bargain, but I know it's not costing him nothing out of his own pocket.

"After I debrief you," he replies.

I put on a show of reluctance, but man, I'm in a hurry to get Patricia out of here before she cracks wide open.

"Okay, let's do it."

Without even the slightest ghost of a smile in triumph, he says, "Tell me about the stolen pharmacy drugs."

I say, "What do you want to know?"

He says, "Everything."

Okay, so I give him the names of all those young guys cutting their way through pharmacy roofs to avoid the burglar alarms, then peeling the safe, if it's an old one, to get the Schedule Two narcotics, and finally doing a smash and grab on the locked cabinets to get the other stuff. All them guys that brought their drug loot to me to find out what they had. Naturally, they didn't bring me the morphine and Demerol products cuz they could figure them out for themselves, but pills with long chemical names, those they needed some help on.

I'm telling you, these guys were too stupid to latch onto a PDR, that's a *Physician's Desk Reference*, in case you didn't know. The book's got photos of all the drugs, plus it says what the drugs are for. Anybody wants one can buy a copy at most large bookstores. But rather than fork over the thirty, forty bucks myself, I just steal my copy of the PDR from a different public library every year. In any case, you can see how dumb these burglars are, so it's like I'm doing the world a favor by getting these beginning criminals off the street before they get into something bad and maybe hurt a civilian or two. And, I'm doing my part with the cops just like they asked. Even a straight citizen like you should appreciate my efforts.

Yeah, sure, I'll take another drink. Make it a double while you're at it.

So, I get done with giving Detective Morales all the names and dates and addresses and the pharmacies that got knocked off. When he finally quits writing, he looks up at me again and says in that deadpan voice of his, "Tell me about the other stuff."

Now, I'm not sure what other stuff he's talking about, and I don't wanna cough up on myself if I don't have to.

"What other stuff?" I ask.

He fixes those cop eyes on me and I'm thinking, "Oh crap."

"The burglar teams you ran yourself."

How in the hell did he find that out? Somebody really close to me has evidently been ratting me out. It can't be Patricia cuz I never told her about those jobs. Besides, I never entered a pharmacy myself on a burglary. I made sure I wasn't anywhere in the neighborhood when those things happened. No, what I did way back then was to take in a couple of young runaways and let them sleep on the floor in my living room. I took them off the streets where they might get hurt, and I fed them. I was doing a Good Samaritan thing until they were able to take care of themselves on their own.

Naturally these kids needed money, so I suggested that they get jobs in some drug store or discount big box with a pharmacy inside, even if all they did was sweep floors. You, being a civilian, would be surprised how easy it is to get alarm codes and make impressions of all the right keys when you've got somebody working on the inside. And you know, the minds of them young runaways are pretty pliable when they're hungry. After a while, they get to thinking they owe you for all your generosity in putting them up when they had nothing to live on.

So, like I said, I never burglarized a pharmacy in my life and I never forced anybody to do it for me. All I did was suggest to those kids how they could do it themselves, if they had a mind to and were looking for some quick cash. After that, it was their own free choice. So, they made some money, and I made some money, more than my usual ten percent with those other idiots. Everybody was happy. After a few jobs, the kids went their separate way and I started over with a fresh bunch of runaways. Guess you could say I was pumping new cash into the local economy. The only people got hurt were the insurance companies, and we all know they're already rich, so what's the harm?

Anyway, this is the other stuff that Detective Morales wanted to hear about. I didn't know how much of the details Morales already knew, and he's gonna revoke my cooperation-and-walk deal if he catches me in a lie. So, once we settle the immunity for me question, I tell him pretty much everything, except I put it in the best light possible for me. I don't wanna look too bad here, or else he might change his mind and somehow queer the deal on my walk. I give him every last name, date and detail of pharmacy burglaries that those young runaways did. I mean, now that I'm caught, it's my civic duty to cooperate with the government, right? Guess you could look at my part as it takes a criminal to catch a criminal, so I'm doing my part the best I know how.

Of course I did feel kinda bad later about a couple of those runaways. I really liked them. But what could I do? My back was against the wall because somebody else had already informed on *me*. And you know, I see my situation being the same as the knocked over dominoes theory. I got bumped and knocked over, and now it's my turn to pass on the bump to the next guy standing close to me. It's the way them vice cops work, only when they bump a guy, they expect him to bump at least five or six guys to take his place in the line. It's one of them mathematical progression things.

But, yeah, I heard later that when the cops went to arrest one of the runaways I liked, the kid had a handgun on him and didn't come out so good. That's the problem with violence, somebody's gonna get hurt, and that's why I don't have nothing to do with guns. Most of the time, anyway.

I didn't go to the funeral or nothing, but me and a couple of my associates did have a party at my place to honor the dead guy. It was the least we could do.

Speaking of partying, if you're still buying drinks then I'll keep on talking about this snitch thing, as you call it. Yeah, another double is good.

Anyway, I give Detective Morales everything, and he says he'll write me up with a cooperating individual number so my name won't appear in any of the reports. Says that's how they protect their informants. Sounds great to me, no exposure, no problems. He has me sign my statement while one of the other detectives comes in and acts as a witness on the signature line. Then Morales photographs me, rolls my fingerprints and takes a personal history for their informant files. Now he knows all my relatives and close friends, even that piddling checking account me and Patricia have down at the corner bank. There's nowhere I can go and hide from these guys if something goes wrong, but then I figure now I'm safe, I don't need to hide from the law. Maybe I'll get a real job and straighten out my life. Maybe even get Patricia off drugs. Do her some good, she's starting to look a little haggard anyway.

Life's looking up.

Two months later, the cops haul me into a Grand Jury and I get to recite my story all over again. If I somehow leave something out, and I'll admit a couple of events slipped my mind, then the damn prosecutor has that signed statement I gave to Detective Morales right there in his hot little hands to help my recollection. Man, by the time I got out of there, I'm sweating like the backup pig at a Hawaiian luau. It was grim. I never had my memory refreshed so many times in my life.

So now I figure the vice detectives will go out and arrest everybody I just testified against, them guys will all make the best plea deal they can to keep their prison time down, and that's that. Of course, I'll have to be careful not to get caught in any more crimes, cuz me getting put in the same cell with one of them boys probably wouldn't be good for my health. Sure, the defense attorneys don't have my name, just a cooperating individual number on the police reports as to who did what, but with all the extra time for thinking some of those boys will have for the next several years, believe me, they'll be putting two and two together. I'll have to think of a new line of work to make money on the streets, something that don't put me at this kind of risk no more.

Come nine months later, Patricia is pretty well off drugs. She can't buy none, nowhere. Hardly anybody will even sell to me, especially if they've heard about us. But then we didn't have much money to be buying drugs with anyway. I'm pretty much out of the business. Seems the word on the street is that we're both narcs. One of the boys in the can must've done his math, and then put the word to the outside. Now the rest of the druggies are too paranoid to have anything to do with yours truly. Good thing I recently found a new scam to make money, otherwise we'd have to leave town.

Then it all goes south. One of the older boys, Billy, had a couple of priors I didn't know about. The prosecutor is lining up to try Billy as an adult. This time Billy can't make a good deal on his charges, so he wants a trial. What's he got to lose? I also hear on the grapevine that some of the boys can't believe it's me that gave them up, so by Billy going to trial, he gets to face his accuser. No more CI numbers on police reports. Now, I get dragged in to testify in open court. And this damn judge lets TV cameras operate inside his court room. What kind of crazy deal is that? The man must be running for political office or something. I know it sure blew my deniability factor to anybody who wasn't sitting right there in the court room. Yeah, I could lie all day to my buds on the street, but there was no way I could get my face back off that camera so who's gonna believe me?

Hey, I got it, on TV is where you saw me, wasn't it? You recognized my face from the TV screen, and that's why you called me a snitch. Yeah, I thought so. But since you're buying me all them drinks and listening to my story, let's don't worry about any prior hard feelings on my part at the start of our little conversation. You just didn't understand the situation at the time.

Anyway, I sat in that damn witness chair for two full days. Let me tell you, they don't call it the hot seat for nothing. That defense attorney called me everything but a human being. I don't ever want to get involved in one of these type situations again. And that's pretty much my story. As you can see, being a cooperating individual is a dangerous occupation, and it definitely screws up your social life.

#

"Another bar, down by the river, where the drinks are cheaper? Sure, as long as it's a short walk. I don't want to lose this buzz. And as long as you're buying, yeah, I'll keep on telling stories about the street. No problem.

"One funny thing I got to tell you though. When you didn't have enough cash in your pockets to cover our bar bill and you had to use plastic, I was looking over your shoulder at the name on your credit card. The ironic thing is, and you'll get a kick out of this, you got the same last name as that young pharmacy burglar that had a gun and the cops shot him dead. Life sure has some strange coincidences, don't it?"

#

Walk with this guy down by the river? Okay, that was my plan in the beginning, but I'm not completely stupid. What the hell's he thinking here? It's dark down there with all the street lights what are shot out and the city being slow to replace. This whole situation is starting to give me them old paranoia feelings again, playing with the inside of my head, like bugs buzzing around in a clear glass jar.

Something ain't totally kosher about this old guy. He don't dress right to be in a place like this, and he don't talk street like us. For him to be buying me all them drinks, he wants something. We'll just have to see what's on his mind. Now if he's looking for one of them alternative lifestyle things, then it's gonna be a rude awakening for him, cuz he done hit on the wrong boy. I ain't that way as he'll soon find out.

Of course, if'n Patricia was here, she'd say it's just all them drugs I scrounged lately giving me the paranoids like they usually do, but I've survived a long time on these streets by listening to that little warning voice in my head. When that old man can't see what I'm doing, I'm gonna slide my right hand under my shirttail and around to the back of my waistband. Make sure my hidden Beretta isn't gonna snag up on my clothes when I need it quick. And, I will.

"Take everything you can," is my new first rule of business. If they don't have cash, then jewelry and plastic will do. Secondly, "be prepared for anything," has always been my back up guide to keep me walking safe.

Survival.

Out here, on the street, you never know what's coming at you... 'til it gets here

SHEPHERD OF THE VALLEY

Do you believe what you see with your own eyes, feel with your own hands, even if you know it's irrational? Or do you lock this knowledge away inside your head and never speak of it again? Not to anyone.

#

I drank more now to forget the war, but booze didn't work the way it used to. After coming home from Belleau Wood and the Argonne Forest, the juice had done its job, however lately, that liquid embrace of eighty proof which allowed me to drift off into the welcoming arms of Morpheus had acquired a different effect. I still needed it to get to sleep, but this constant self-medication also relaxed any tight control I kept on my thoughts. Not good for business when you're struggling to survive as a private detective.

For sanity's sake, I had compartmentalized my brain. Dark, violent memories got locked away in mental closets,

closets I never intentionally opened. Unfortunately, that wonderful sleep elixir began to numb my inner guard, loosened hinges on some of them locked doors. On those nights, howling, half-glimpsed terrors prowled the corridors of my mind and I awoke in a cold sweat reaching for the gun under my pillow.

After one of those nightmares, I usually added a little extra to my coffee to smooth out the morning. I wasn't supposed to sleep here in my one room office, but sometimes it wasn't worth going back to my bed at the boarding house. And, since the old biddy of a house proprietor had strict rules against drinking anywhere on her property, I kept a bottle of bourbon in the lower right hand desk drawer in my office. The Volstead Act may have been the law of the land, but most folks broke that law daily. Being a criminal these days was all in how you looked at it.

I poured amber liquid into my coffee until the bottle gurgled twice, then screwed the cap back on and put it away. Sipping at the steaming black mixture, I went over the testimony I was scheduled to give in court this morning. Not much time to get ready. Hands on my pocket watch only gave me about half an hour to shape up and make my way through the cold gusts of autumn wind outside and over to the county court house. Concentrating on my hand scribbled notes wasn't the easiest thing to do right now, but I tried.

Almost missed the knock at my door. The sound came gentle and hesitant.

Turning the large brass key in the lock, I swung the door open and got an eyeful of womanhood, the kind that gave a man something to think about on cold, lonely nights. Being so easy to look at, I took my time. She actually blushed a little before recovering herself. I put her at late twenties, early thirties, not beautiful, but pretty in a handsome way. Her long black coat, showing wear at the bottom hem and both sleeve cuffs, hung unbuttoned in front. I reminded myself to keep my gaze above her neck line, at least until I found out the score, but good intentions seldom last long.

The dress she wore underneath appeared homemade out of cheap cloth, while her shoes were working class. No money to be had here, I told myself, just the possibility of pleasant company for a while.

Speaking softly, but a little on the husky side, she inquired. "You Frank Jubal?"

Her accent definitely sounded West Virginia, but more than that, it was mountain people. Probably some snake bend in the river of one of those steep walled valleys where they mined coal.

I took a harder look.

She had a Celtic face, hair as black as a raven's back and the green eyes of a cat just staring at me. Black Irish came to mind, probably third generation over here. On my first perusal I'd missed the dark smudges ground into her shoe leather. They had the stain of coal dust on 'em.

"Yes ma'am, that's me, but you'd best know I don't work for script. There's nothing I want to buy in some coal mine company store."

"I can pay in dollars," she replied.

Ah yes, the magic words of admittance.

"Come on in."

She took the straight back chair in front of my desk while I sat in a swivel on the opposite side of the scarred oak top, doing my best to look professional in a wrinkled suit and slightly stained vest. I buttoned my collar and straightened my tie. Time to earn some of them dollars she'd mentioned.

"What can I do for you, Ma'am?"

Her answer was blunt and to the point. "I need someone to protect my husband."

I mulled that over. Lots of miners were at war with strike breakers hired by the coal mines. Union organizers had their work cut out for them in this part of the country. Hadn't been that many years since the losers of the Matewan Massacre and the Battle of Blair Mountain got buried. Not to mention other killings on a smaller scale. Seemed like everybody carried guns these days. Of course the governor had calmed some of the shooting by calling in the National Guard, yet thugs from the Baldwin-Felts Detective Agency working for the mine owners still operated with a free hand in company owned towns, and they had a lot more man power than me. Not circumstances I wanted to risk my neck in, leastwise not times when I had full control on my mind. Might have to take a pass on this job.

"Ma'am, I'm not big enough to go up against goons the mines hire to keep out unions."

My comment didn't seem to bother her none. She just sat there on the front of her chair, knees pressed together, hands in her lap clutching her purse, and her back as rigid as a hickory broom handle. There was a slight edge to this woman if you knew what to look for.

"Call me Missus Bates, if you don't mind. My first name is Fannie, and Charlie Bates is my husband. In our valley, all the mines are family owned and run. We never sold our land out to the big companies like others did."

That statement made the prospect of me taking on this piece of work a little easier.

"Then who would I be protecting your husband from?"

Her gaze shifted away, and for the first time I detected

a slight tremor in her hands.

"I'm not really sure."

That should have clued me in that something wasn't right. Clients requesting a bodyguard usually knew who meant them harm.

I tried a different tact.

"What makes you think Charlie's in danger?"

She chose her words carefully. "Three of his close friends in the valley have been murdered recently, slashed to death. A couple others have disappeared. My husband, when he's drinking, talks like him and the rest of his crowd are next on the list."

"The list?"

"Well, there's not a written list that anyone actually knows of, but I'd say somebody's crossing off a list of names in his head."

I glanced at my pocket watch. Almost time for court to start, with me being the star witness in a big time bunco case.

"Ma'am, uh, Missus Bates, we aren't talking about one of them old time family feuds here are we?"

Her eyes came round to my gaze again.

"Mister Jubal, all the mining families in our hollow pretty well know each other and there's no bad blood, at least not the killing kind amongst them."

Another glance at my watch. If I hurried, I could still make it without getting cross-wise with the judge. I stood up to leave.

"I'll be in court today and tomorrow, after that I'm free to take on any new assignment."

She hesitated only long enough for me to think I'd lost the job, but then, "If that's the best we can get, I'll take it. Just hurry for my husband's sake."

"Sure," I said. "Tell me where to find your place, plus

I'll need a retainer."

As she dug through her purse, she gave me directions to the valley and dirt road leading up to their place. Then, out of a clasp top coin purse, she extracted a wad of crumpled dollar bills.

I saw some ones, fives and a ten, enough to get me hired anyway. Scooping up the money, I showed her out the door. Gave her my phone number and said I'd be at her place in two days. Then I locked up the office and headed for the stairs. I'd get more details on the job from her later. That was my plan anyway.

#

The following evening after court was recessed and the jury went into deliberations, I got a phone call from a John Bates. Said as Charlie's brother he was calling in place of Missus Bates, and there was no longer any sense for me to be in a hurry. Said Charlie was already dead and they were burying him the next day.

"What happened?" I asked.

"Mister Jubal," came the reply, "I'm calling long distance from the general store and I don't have that kind of money for an extended conversation. You want to know what happened, come on down and see for yourself. As I understand it, the widow already paid you some, for all the good it did Charlie."

Then he hung up.

He was right, I had the money. And now the job was finished before it started. I could just keep the cash and go on to whatever other work came my way. Or I could return all them wrinkled dollar bills to the recent widow. I sipped whiskey dregs from my coffee mug and thought about it. She was worth seeing again, which led me to my third option. I could just drive over there, like the man said, and see what was going on. Damn, why not? I put the bottle away.

The rest of the evening was spent oiling my .45 automatic and getting things ready. As a last minute thought, I unlocked the closet in my office and dragged out my old Army foot locker. Stashed inside was the Browning Automatic Rifle I'd smuggled onto the troop ship when the remnants of our infantry company came home from France. This piece of cold, unthinking steel had been my one constant companion in the trenches and muddy fields of Europe, and had saved my life more than once. Probably wouldn't need it where I was headed, but my mind was more at ease just for having it along. To my way of thinking, this BAR was one of the few reliable friends I had left.

I slept in the office again, but the bottle remained in the drawer. This night passed without bringing the dreams which usually haunted my mind. Instead, I slept like the innocent, no monsters lurking in the corridor, no Angel of Death whispering in my ear, no cold sweat. For some reason, the closet doors stayed firmly locked. It was almost like being human again.

Before the sun climbed over the mountain ridge, I packed my Model T Ford and followed the directions Missus Bates had given me. Three hours later, I came to the turnoff. A single road led into the narrow valley, a road cut deep into the slope of one steep wall. Far down below, angry water coursed around giant boulders long ago fallen into the bottom of the winding dark river. Wouldn't do for an automobile to go wide in one of these curves and drop over the edge.

After a few miles, the town she'd mentioned came into view. It didn't consist of much more than a general store, a couple other buildings and some scattered houses. All of them looked well weathered and could do with repairs and a coat of paint. Said something about the local prosperity. Made me wonder where Fannie Bates got all them crumpled dollars.

I was looking for the road out to the Bates place when a board sign swinging in the autumn wind caught my attention. The paint may have faded, but the words were still legible. Seemed somebody by the last name of Morden claimed to be a doctor in these parts. He also operated as dentist, coroner and several other odd jobs the sign alleged he was qualified to perform. I pulled my Ford over in front of his white picket gate and got out.

A sidewalk cobbled together of rough boards led up to the porch. His front steps squeaked and the porch had a soft spot in the boards. The doctoring business couldn't have been much of a going concern.

He answered the door on my third knock. From the looks of his short chubby body, flushed cheeks and foreign clothes, he didn't appear to be from the same ethnic stock that made up this mining community.

"You the doctor?" I inquired.

"Ya, I am. You need help?"

"You bet. I see by the sign out front that you're also the coroner in these parts. I need to ask you about a dead man."

He stared at me for a while as if trying to make up his mind about something.

"We've had several dead men recently."

"So I've heard. Tell me about Charlie Bates."

"You are *polizei?*"

"Huh?"

"I believe you call it police."

"No, I'm not the police."

He crooked his head to one side and looked up at me.

"Ah, you are the man Missus Bates hired to protect Charlie?"

I didn't much like having my failure thrown in my face, but other than that this little Kraut had the circumstances right.

"Just tell me about Charlie."

He led me into his waiting room and related the story of Charlie's last evening. Missus Bates had fed Charlie supper, and then he'd stepped out on his back porch for an evening smoke. She cleared the table and started washing dishes. Hearing some screams, Missus Bates grabbed a kerosene lantern and rushed out the back door. She found Charlie lying in a pool of blood."

"How'd he die?"

"His face, throat, chest and abdomen were severely slashed."

"Knife?"

Doc Morden lit his Meerschaum pipe and took a deep drag. Tendrils of white smoke snaked up toward the ceiling.

"Most of those cuts were too parallel to have been done by a man with a knife."

"Then what?"

He smoked for a while as if considering how to put his words.

"As a boy in my village outside the Black Forest, I saw... But, no, I didn't believe it then and I don't believe it now."

"You're leaving me hanging here, Doc. I need something to go on."

For a fat man, he moved pretty fast. Springing out of his chair, he grabbed his coat and motioned to me.

"Come, you haff an automobile and our circuit rider will soon be starting the funeral. Let him and the family tell you what they know and what they think."

A mile outside of town, the road began to climb again. When we got to several vehicles parked along the road's edge, I turned around, pulled over to one side and set the hand brake. We both got out.

Over the lip of the road and slightly downhill was an open meadow with several people making their way down slope. Six of them carried a rectangular pine box on their shoulders. Others followed behind. A solitary figure dressed in a black suit and wearing a large brimmed, floppy black hat pulled low over his forehead seemed to be standing at the head of an open grave waiting for the procession to come down. I took him for the circuit rider.

Doc Morden and I started down the hill. Turned out not everyone was attending graveside services. I noticed a grey-bearded man perched on a small boulder just down from the road's edge. He had one of those old-time muzzle loaders resting across his lap and his head kept slowly swiveling to sweep the meadow from one side to the other. His eyes finally settled on Doc and me. When he caught me staring back at him, he nodded, but said nothing.

"Who's that?" I asked.

"Dat's Charlie's Vater-in-law."

"Doesn't look like he's going to the funeral. What's the matter, didn't he like Charlie?"

"Oh, he like Charlie fine. I joost think he has other concerns on his mind."

Before I could ask any more questions, I had to catch up with the damn little Kraut. For a short, fat guy he walked fast. By the time I caught up, we were at the back of the small crowd of mourners, the widow Bates stood numbly at the foot of the freshly dug hole in the ground and the traveling preacher had started his service.

"Yeah, though I walk..." his voice intoned.

I'd been to several funerals a few years back, all for buddies who weren't coming home from the Great War, so I could tell it would be a while before I could talk to people at this one. I let my mind and eyes wander across the group as the pall bearers slowly lowered the casket on twisted hemp ropes.

"...through the Valley...," came the preacher's words. In the cold shaft of late afternoon sunlight, that tall, lean figure in the black frock coat read from a worn Bible half concealed in his large, hairy hands. "...of the Shadow of Death..."

The thud of the casket hitting bottom startled me, but then I'd been contemplating my own Angel of Death who haunted my frequent nightmares.

"...I shall fear..."

Three pall bearers drew the loose rope ends up out of the grave, and then walked around to join the rest of the mourners. That deep slash in the ground and the odor of raw earth reminded me of the deadly trenches I'd spent so much time in, yet I had managed to come out of those trenches alive. No way was Charlie coming out of this one. I felt the urge for a drink.

"...no evil..."

For some reason, the gravelly voice of the circuit rider seemed to have stirred up the mourners. Several of the lean, hard men shuffled their feet restlessly and bent forward slightly like they were trying to see under the preacher's broad brimmed hat. I noticed two men whose hands strayed toward the waist of their suit coats as if reaching for something at their belts. I stepped to the front rank to get a better look at whatever was bothering them.

"...for I am..."

Closing the Bible and speaking as though from memory, the preacher stepped around to the far side of the grave and pressed the black bound book into the widow's hands. Then, interlacing his long hairy fingers and cracking his knuckles, he finished the litany in a rough voice growing with excitement.

"...the Death in this valley."

Suddenly, he cast his hat aside and pivoted his ears forward.

For one shocked heartbeat, no one moved. Then Missus Bates screamed and someone trying to get away pushed me hard from behind. I landed face down on the casket and quickly rolled onto my back just in time to catch the widow as she fainted and pitched forward. Her weight pinned my right arm against my chest. Something large and black leaped across the open mouth of the grave, but I was busy trying to roll Missus Bates off to the side with one hand and yank my .45 loose from my shoulder holster with the other.

The sounds of running feet reached back to my ears. Judging by the screams I heard, at least two of the mourners weren't quick enough. The screams died away.

Silence.

Then a snuffling noise slowly worked its way over to the lip of the grave.

Still trapped lying on my back, I thumbed the safety off and waited in the sudden quiet. With four open sides to this tomb I couldn't cover all of them. Loose dirt fell into the grave.

There.

A silhouette appeared above the top of my head. Even though I was looking at it from upside down, I swung the .45 up over my forehead and emptied the magazine until the slide locked in place. Hot, ejected brass shells bounced around inside the dirt enclosure, burning my neck and right cheek.

The figure disappeared.

I cocked my head and listened. Nothing but a loud ringing in my ears.

I popped out the worthless magazine and jammed in a loaded one, released the slide with my thumb and felt the cartridge ram home in the breech. With the hammer cocked and ready, I got my legs under me, cautiously stood up on the casket and took stock of the outside world.

At the head of the grave, a small pool of red seeped its way into the hungry earth. Further out, blood spatter made a trail leading away toward a nearby wood.

I spun in a quick circle. Whatever evil had been here was gone, but he'd left his handiwork behind. On the uphill side of my earthen trench, lay the sprawled bodies of two pall bearers. They didn't move, not even a twitch, but from the great amount of blood soaking into their clothes that was understandable. I'd been one lucky S.O.B. this time around.

Way up the slope, the survivors still ran for their lives. A certain doctor with his short legs led the pack. No telling who'd pushed me in the back. I lowered my pistol.

It took some effort, but I finally lifted Fannie's unconscious body out of the grave and carried her up slope to the road. Here, I found the fat little doctor in a panic. He was sitting in the driver's seat of my automobile trying to start the motor but forgetting to use the choke. I dropped Missus Bates onto the front passenger seat, grabbed the doctor by his left suit lapel and turned him to face me. Somebody had a lot of questions to answer. I'd start with him.

"What the hell was that thing?"

"A werewolf," he screamed. "I've suspected that for some time in these murders."

I don't know what I'd expected to hear, but it wasn't that.

"You're crazy, that's stuff for scary stories on dark nights. This is broad daylight and it won't be a full moon for several days yet."

"What are you going to believe," the doctor screamed back, "logic, or your own eyes?"

I punched him alongside the head once to knock any nonsense out of his brain, then slapped both cheeks lightly to get his attention back.

"Look, Doc, here's what you're going to do."

I cupped both of his cheeks in my hands so he had to focus on me.

"First, you're going to use the choke so the motor starts, then you're going to drive Missus Bates to your house and take care of her until I get there. Understand?"

I nodded his head for him in agreement.

"Good. Now I'm going to get something out of the back seat and then you can leave."

I'd barely retrieved my BAR wrapped up in a blanket from the back seat before Doc got the motor roaring and ready. The rear door slammed itself as he pulled away with a jerk.

One glance at the sun told me I still had a few hours of daylight. Tracking wild beasts wasn't my area of expertise, but hell, anybody could've followed that blood trail. In ten minutes, I was deep in the mountain forest and totally out of my realm. The blood spots got further and further apart, and I found myself shying at every rustle of dead leaves, every breaking branch on the ground.

Penetrating shafts of sunlight grew scarce in this thick underbrush as the sun rotated west. Wind knocked the tops of trees together in weird clacking noises like swinging skeleton bones. I paused to catch my breath and glanced up from the trail.

He stood just off the path and behind the thick trunk of a fallen dead tree, watching me.

Automatically, I swung the BAR in his direction.

"You spoiled my shot back there, son."

Damn. I moved my front sight away from the old greybeard's mid-section and eased off on the trigger. His ancient muzzle loader stayed pointed at the sky.

"What do you mean?"

"I had that creature dead center. When you popped off a few rounds with your pistol, you winged him in the shoulder and spun him sideways. Made my shot go wide. Now we have to hunt him down."

"What exactly are we hunting here, old man? Doc Morden called it a werewolf, but I'll tell you right now, I don't believe a man can suddenly metamorphose into a wolf. That's too big a change."

The old man chuckled, but it wasn't meant as humor.

"You're right, son, that thing didn't have a sudden change. I'll tell you what I heard and what I know for sure, and then you believe what you want to."

I nodded my head in agreement.

"Indians tell stories about the migration of their tribe into these mountains long ago. They found a people already living here, wild people with strange rituals and animal powers, not like you and I at all. The tribe came to fear these people and hunted them down until there was only one left, a witch woman who retreated into a valley where many of the trees had been blown down in a great windstorm. It was one valley the tribe found unsafe to venture into. But, on nights with full moonlight, the witch woman could sometimes be seen running through the forests with a pack of silvertip wolves."

"Nice story, old man, but what's that got to do with this creature we're hunting?"

"Some say the witch woman bore fruit. Long after that, some of the tribe's young women disappeared, and shapes of those running in the wolf pack slowly began to change from one generation to the next. You figure it out."

"You're saying this creature is part human, part wolf?"

"I'd guess this one's at least seven-eighths human or more by now."

"Not possible."

"I'm a creationist myself," replied the old man, "believe in the Good Book. But, I'm willing to concede maybe that scientist from England stumbled on to something about survival and evolution of the species. These beasts have certainly evolved some even in my lifetime. Tell me you haven't run across strange creatures yourself out there in the world, animals that don't fit the mold."

I wasn't going to argue religion and science with the old man. All I wanted to do was kill this thing and go home.

"So, why'd he start killing coal miners?"

"About eighteen years back when Charlie Bates was a young boy, his dad and a bunch of other hunters wandered into Deadfall Valley looking for deer. Charlie and his friends tagged along. The party discovered a log cabin front built over the mouth of a cave. Inside was a half eaten deer carcass and some of these wolf-like creatures. The hunters slaughtered all the creatures except for one, a young pup. They took it back as a hunting trophy. Charlie's dad also skinned one of the dead beasts and stretched its hide on the side of his barn."

"What happened to the young'un?"

"Call it one of them twists in human nature. Seems our

circuit rider's wife was barren, no hope for family. When the hunting party showed off their trophy, she begged to have him. The pup did look pretty much human at the time. So, I took pity on the woman and promised several jars of moonshine to Charlie's dad if they gave her the pup."

"You're a moonshiner?"

"Best in these hills."

"That's where Fannie got the money to pay me?"

"Yep."

"And that pup you saved grew up to kill Charlie?"

The old man rested his muzzle loader in the crook of his arm.

"My fault, but I aim to rectify it real soon."

"Where'd everything go wrong?"

"Preacher didn't take kindly to the young'un, considered him spawn of the devil. Took to beating the boy in later years when he was slow to learn scripture. Didn't help none that Charlie's crowd picked on the young'un. Then one day, preacher discovered the little whelp was growing a tail. Took him out to the barn and chopped it off with an axe. The creature ran away and we thought that was the end of it."

"Until the killings started."

I wasn't sure the old man heard my last statement. He appeared to be studying the slow creep of sunrays across the forest floor.

"It'll be dark in a couple of hours," he said. "If you're rested, we'd best be moving." Without waiting for me, he took up the trail again.

With all the dead fallen tree trunks we had to scramble over, I had trouble keeping up.

"What is this place?"

"Deadfall Valley," he whispered back, "now be quiet

or stay behind."

A few miles later, with about an hour of sunlight left, we bellied down onto a ridge overlooking a small meadow. The old man put his lips next to my ear and murmured. "Stay here and shoot anything that crosses that open space. I'll be off to your right a ways." Then he was gone. I scarce heard him leave, but then I still had a low ringing in my ears from earlier.

I extended the bipod on my BAR and wriggled my knees and elbows into the soft parts of the earth to make a comfortable shooting position. By sighting down the barrel, I could cover most of the open ground down slope. Nothing moved in front of me except the tall brown stalks of dead grass rippling in waves from cooling winds. Time dragged on. My eyes grew tired of straining.

As the sun lowered behind me, rays of light fell on the front of a log cabin almost concealed in the trees at the far side of the meadow. Inside the cabin, something stirred, came to the doorway, left, then returned again to look out.

I adjusted my sights to compensate for the extra distance.

A figure came out of the cabin and as far as the tree line. It walked upright, but then so had the creature we now hunted. Damn, I should've brought binoculars.

As it came into the open meadow, I saw it wore a black frock coat and large brimmed floppy hat, but at this distance I wasn't sure it was our quarry. Somehow, it seemed smaller and slightly different than our fake preacher at the grave site. Couldn't be sure. I waited for the old grey-beard off to my right to take the first shot.

The figure started across the meadow and toward the ridge I was lying on. Still the old man didn't shoot and I couldn't tell if this thing coming my way was man or beast.

I eased the safety on my automatic rifle to OFF. The old man had said to shoot anything that crossed the meadow. He'd better be right. My finger took up slack in the trigger. I centered the sight.

BOOM!

From further up the ridge, the old man's muzzle loader exploded.

The figure in the meadow crumpled and fell.

I removed my finger from the trigger and popped my head up for a better view.

That's when, on the ground directly around the shadow of my head, I saw another rapidly growing shadow. Something was creeping up behind me. As the shadow leaped, I rolled over and tried to swing the BAR into shooting position, but the creature was too close.

I held the rifle at arm's length as a barrier between us. Claws slashed toward my neck, barely grazing the skin. My right hand turned loose of the rifle stock and scrambled for the .45 in my shoulder holster.

The beast beat down my left arm and the rifle that shielded me. He threw himself on my chest. Teeth reached for soft tissue at my throat.

I pointed the .45 in the direction of his chest and pulled the trigger as fast as I could. Someone kept screaming in the background, and I hoped it was me, cuz if it was, then that meant I was still alive.

The weight on my chest panicked me. I kicked my way out from under and scurried crabwise until my backside came up against a tree. The screaming had stopped. Other than that, the loud ringing was back in my ears.

Afterward, the old man was lucky I was out of bullets, or I'd have shot him too when he wandered out of the trees along the ridge.

"With all that screaming," he said, "I wasn't sure what

I'd find when I got over here, but it looks like we both shot one."

He rolled over the creature I'd blown holes in and removed the floppy hat on its head. "Yep, that's our fake preacher. I expect we'll find the real one dead somewhere else."

I wasn't in any mental condition for rational conversation about now, and I'll admit that most of the remaining evening was a blur. I do remember going down into the meadow and seeing the other creature up close. And I remember the old man dragging both bodies into the cabin and setting fire to the place. The trip back to the old man's stake bed truck at the cemetery was a stumbling nightmare in the dark. Eventually, a half moon rose over the mountains, which was better than no light to walk by.

My next memory was me turning the hand crank on the truck motor while the old man sat inside the cab and worked the throttle. It didn't start on the first crank. As I got ready to try again, there was a howl in the distance. I froze.

"Did you hear that?"

The old man pocked his head out of the cab. "Hear what?"

"That wolf howl."

"Nope, can't hear nothing in here with all that wind. Give her another crank."

I put a lot more muscle into it this time and the motor fired up. The old man didn't have to tell me twice to get in. I slammed the door and pointed the BAR out the window all the way back to town.

We stopped briefly at Doc Morden's house, but only for me to get my Model T. I may or may not have said goodbye to the widow Bates, then I was down the road. At least once going through some of those treacherous curves, I recall hearing another haunting wolf howl floating down from the steep valley walls. I increased my speed.

Wasn't long after that I let my room at the boarding house go, too many doors and windows in the place. Do all my sleeping at the office now where there's just one way in. These days, I only take daylight jobs, getting back to the office before dark. And the bottle in my right hand desk drawer stays there, untouched.

There's monsters in dreams that make you sweat, and there's that thing out there I don't talk about to nobody else. Who'd believe me without those two corpses as proof? But I know there's got to be at least one more of them things out there. Somehow me and the old man missed running into him that evening, so my advice to everyone now is don't come messing around my office door late at night, cuz my Browning Automatic Rifle stays right there on my desk top, within easy reach.

I don't much care, you believe what you want.

ABSOLUTION

It was on Luis Rubio's mind that maybe now would be a good time to seek absolution. The way things were headed, there might not be a chance for such niceties later. And, that was how he came to find himself kneeling inside a small, closet sized room with a curtain for a door, while he considered where his future was going.

A polite cough coming from the other side of the screen in the front wall made Luis suddenly realize this wasn't the first such noise from the other compartment. His thoughts must've drifted and now he needed to bring them back to the present. Events of this past afternoon would catch up with him soon enough.

"*Lo siento, padre*, I have much on my mind and did not hear you come in."

"You have many great sins to confess?"

Luis had to think about that for a moment. This priest seemed to have a young voice, but Luis didn't know if that was good or bad for his purpose here this evening.

"No, I think all my prior transgressions have been

small ones. It's just that I haven't been inside a church for a very long time."

"How long has it been since your last confession?"

Luis pursed his lips and rolled his eyes upward as though to find the correct answer somewhere in the front of his brain.

"I think I was about ten years of age. That's when my mother died."

"Your mother had a church burial?"

"Yes."

"But your father didn't bring you to church after that?" inquired the priest.

"No," Luis replied, "my father was very much involved in the family business with my two uncles in those days."

"What sort of business keeps a man from coming to church?"

"My father and his two elder brothers were coyotes. I'm sure you've heard many desperate prayers over the years from our people who wished for a better life back then, even as they do now. Anyway, someone had to show them the way north, how to avoid the Border Patrol. It can be a long journey from Ciudad Juarez when one has to walk far around the barriers, and weekends were usually the best times for them to go."

There was silence for a while on the other side of the screen.

Then.

"So tell me why you are here now. What do you wish of me?"

"I would like forgiveness for those sins I may have committed in the past. It would be good if I could start over with a clean slate so I'm not judged too harshly at the end."

"Very well, tell me of your wrongdoing to others and

we will proceed from there."

Luis thought back in time before reciting a short list of his failings. He tried to get it all in, but other than smuggling people into Los Estados Unidos, an occupation which he considered to be a practical solution to his country's unemployment problem rather than a sin, he considered himself to have led a pretty quiet life up to now.

"Is that all?" asked the priest.

"I think so."

"Are there no sins of the flesh?"

Luis hadn't considered that before and hoped it wouldn't be a problem.

"There were a few women, padre, but I don't truly feel sorry for that."

"Still, my son, the church considers lying with a woman outside of the holy bonds of matrimony to be a sin. You must do penance for those transgressions, an act of contrition if you wish to be forgiven."

After a little more thought, Luis decided if that was all it took to clear the slate and have a clear conscience up 'til now, then yeah, he could do some simple penance.

"Okay," he said. "Tell me what I got to do."

The priest hesitated. "We'll get to that in a minute. I sense there's more you haven't told me."

Luis nodded to himself. He had heard from others that such was the trouble with some priests; it was almost like they could see inside a man's thoughts. Perhaps it would be better if he contained himself for a while in order to see how much this young priest actually knew about life in the real world. Yes, he would wait and let matters settle out a bit.

Outside his curtain door, the world held itself mostly quiet as if it too were waiting for something. Occasional footsteps shuffled past on their way to empty pews up front, while muffled prayers of the few faithful in attendance at this evening hour washed softly across the high ceilinged cathedral from one wall to the other and receded in the distance. A faint scent of hot wax, candles lit to invoke the personal help of silent saints, floated on the warm autumn air. Seemed everybody had problems these days, some greater than others.

Still, Luis waited.

"Are you one of us?" the priest finally inquired.

"I was born here twenty-five years ago and later baptized in this very church, if that's what you mean," Luis replied. "But the last time I crossed over the river, I stayed in El Paso and got a job for good money. Three years I worked on a road crew, laying the hot asphalt."

"That is hard work."

"A man does what he has to do to take care of his family. The company over there paid me well."

"And you sent some of this money back home to your family?"

"I did. They needed it to feed the young ones, to buy them shoes and afford to send them to proper schools for an education so they could have a better life."

"A commendable act on your part, but three years is a long time to be gone from loved ones. What brought you back to our side of the river?"

Now they were getting down to it. Luis rubbed at the hollowness inside his chest.

"A party was arranged for my niece's fifteenth birthday. Even though my uncle was very poor, he paid for everything and wished us all to be there for the celebration. This afternoon was to be a fiesta for the whole family."

"Truly a joyous occasion," said the priest.

"Not this one," muttered Luis in a low tone.

"No? What was the problem?"

"Four young men showed up at my uncle's house. They were looking for someone and wanted to know about a new silver car parked on the street just outside my uncle's front door. None of us knew anyone with such a car, and in any case it was only members of our family celebrating inside the house. We knew everyone there, but these men grew angry and accused my uncle of lying."

"What kind of men were they?"

"Hardened men, gangsters, angry at the world. They had bandanas covering their faces and they carried automatic weapons in their hands."

"I see."

"Who knows if these narco terrorists were Zetas, Aztecas, Sinaloa or one of the other cartels? No matter, the result was the same. My uncle tried to assure these men that we knew nothing about the new silver car or its driver, but two of the masked men became enraged and started shooting until their weapons clicked on empty. The red of our blood ran everywhere, the floor, the walls, the furniture. In this one quick massacre I lost everyone in my family. Now it seems I no longer have an anchor to hold me onto the right path in life."

After a short silence, the priest cleared his throat. "There are many paths, my son, and it is up to each of us to choose our own way. I'm sorry for your loss. These are trying times for many of our people."

Luis continued his story as if he hadn't heard.

"My uncle kept a shotgun in a nearby closet. In his older age and failing eyesight, he had long ago sawed a few inches off the barrels to help him bring down birds at a closer range when he was still able to go hunting. And, even though he was severely wounded on this particular day, he managed to shoot that ancient double barrel at least once at the intruders. His bird shot took a wide pattern as the four men scrambled to get out our front door. I remember one of the masked men fell to the floor while another screamed in pain and stumbled outside into the street. I heard this second man cry for help from his companions."

Luis grew silent as he pictured these events in his mind. Yes, that was how one thing had followed another.

"How did *you* manage to survive?" inquired the priest.

"I was in the kitchen when the men entered and asked their questions. By the time I entered the front room where everyone was gathered, the two shooters were almost out of bullets. When they saw me, they hurried their final shots and missed."

"You should say a prayer of thanks, my son. Their bullets missing you was a sign from above."

"More likely the Devil below," Luis murmured.

"No, no," retorted the priest, "the Devil would have no reason to leave you unharmed."

"I have my own thoughts on the matter," said Luis, then he let the conversation lapse again. Eventually, he could hear the priest fidgeting on the other side of the screened opening.

"Then what happened?"

"After my uncle grabbed his old shotgun and fired at the fleeing men, I went to him as quick as I could to see how bad his own wounds were, but he slumped back against the wall and slid down to the floor. He passed before I could help. There was nothing left for me to do, except close his eyes."

"It was good that you were there for him in his final hour," said the priest. "But what of the four masked men? Where did they go?"

"Those first two who got out of the room unharmed came back long enough to help their wounded companion limp across the street after he had cried out in pain. I watched them through the open doorway. They put him into the back seat of a black SUV. Then, they drove off in a hurry. At the time, I didn't know where they were going."

"And the fourth man, the one who fell to the floor, was he dead?"

"I thought so at first, but then he moaned and rolled over on his side."

"Ah, your uncle's bird shot didn't kill him."

"No, but this man was in a very bad way."

"How so?"

"He could barely talk and had no strength to get himself up."

"What did you do?"

"Darkness clouded my mind. I thought about my niece in her new birthday dress, and her youthful blood spattered all over the front of it. That's when I picked up an unfired automatic weapon one of the other masked men had dropped on our floor as he fled through the door. I made sure the safety was off and had my finger hard on the trigger..."

Luis's voice trailed off.

"But you didn't shoot?" inquired the priest.

"No."

"Killing another human being is a mortal sin. It is good you did not pull the trigger."

"At first I wanted very much to kill that man, padre, but then something happened inside of me."

"Surely it was the hand of God that stopped you."

"Don't think so, padre. No, the man's eyes looked up at me and he called my name."

"The man knew you?"

"He called my name, so I laid the killing weapon aside and kneeled down by his head. I removed the bandana to better see his face."

"Did you recognize this man?"

"I did. It was Hector Carrillo. He and I had played together as kids. Back then, we were the best of friends and had even gone to the same school for a few years until Hector dropped out to help his family after his father was killed in a car accident. Yes, I knew him."

"Yet he killed your uncle's family, all your relatives?"

"Hector and I were friends a long time ago. I don't think he knew my uncle, nor that side of my family. When my father was still alive, he always cautioned me not to speak about our family and the business they were in, so I said little about them."

"I see. Did this Hector at least repent of his sins for the killings he helped commit?"

"No, I think he had other things on his mind, things he believed more important to him at that moment."

"More important than the state of his soul? You said he was in a bad way. I assume you meant he was dying."

Luis could see how this young priest could be an excitable man; the tone of the man's speech was reaching up to a higher pitch than was necessary for these circumstances. To Luis' way of thinking it would be better if both of them approached this situation in a calm and logical manner. Besides, time was growing short and he did not wish to become engaged in a long discussion of theology with this priest. All he wanted at this point was to receive absolution for himself, if possible, and then be on his way. He decided to continue this dialogue between them in a softer voice and maybe try to hurry things along a little faster.

"Hector knew things did not look good for his survival, but still he believed he would be okay if I drove him back to the guarded villa of his jefe. He told me his boss had a medical person on the cartel's payroll, a doctor who doesn't ask questions nor whisper in the ear of the local *policia* when a new patient suddenly afflicted with bullet holes shows up at his clinic."

"This killer asked for your help?"

"*Si.*"

"For what possible reason did he think you would help him?"

"Hector said that his *jefe* would pay me ten thousand dollars American money if I brought him safely back to the villa, especially if I also brought along Hector's automatic weapon and their other black SUV which had been left on the street outside our house. Hector had the keys in his pocket. This assistance on my part would be an act of good faith to his boss. After that, he said *el jefe* would put me on the payroll and I could make lots of money in their business."

Luis paused in his telling.

"I must admit, padre, Hector made me look at my immediate future in a different way, one which I had only then conceived of doing. His words showed me the path I must take."

"My son, surely you know such money as this has much blood on it."

"True, padre, but you know as well as I that this same narco blood money has built a religious shrine right here in our city, a shrine that many of the faithful pray at every day. God and the church did nothing to stop the building of this site, and many of our people themselves tend to overlook any stain upon this money. No es verdad?"

The priest cleared his throat.

"Money is the Devil's lure on the road to sin."

Luis Rubio nodded his head.

"That may be, but our government is powerless to put an end to the corruption and violence. Many of our people have simply given up and now just go along in order to survive. It's become a matter of *plata o plomo*, silver or lead. What kind of a choice is that?"

"Still," said the priest, "I cannot believe you would carry out the wishes of this narco assassin."

"Believe," Luis replied, "that I am taking Hector back to the villa of his boss. We will be on our way as soon as you give me absolution."

"Give you absolution?" sputtered the priest. "Your grave sins are yet to come if you persist in going down this violent path where Hector would lead you. But, you cannot ask absolution in advance for acts you may commit in the future. Meanwhile, Hector is the one with black sins hanging heavy on his very soul."

Luis nodded in agreement on that part.

"It's true he has much to atone for."

"I'm glad you at least see that much," said the priest. "Tell me then, is this Hector still alive?"

Luis glanced briefly at the dried blood on his hands.

"He was yet among the living when I saw him last."

The priest sounding impatient now. "Then surely you know where he is. Do you have him with you now?"

"Not here in the church, padre, but he is close by."

There was a scuffing noise on the other side of the screen and then the curtain door on Luis' cubicle was abruptly snatched open. The priest stood in the doorway speaking loudly.

"Take me to him."

Luis rose slowly to his feet.

"As you wish, padre, but I'll take only you, no one else.

And please lower your voice. It would not be good to have a crowd gather and attract notice of the police."

Stepping out of the cubicle, Luis led the priest out of the cathedral, into the night air and down worn steps in front of the church. At the corner, he crossed the intersection and made his way into the shadows along a darker side street. The scuff of shoes on cement told him the priest was close behind. From time to time, Luis looked back over his right shoulder to ensure they weren't being followed by others. Near an alley, he stopped at the side of a black SUV, stepped off the sidewalk and opened the rear passenger door.

The priest stepped forward to peer into the SUV.

"It's too dark in here, I see nothing. Can you give us some light?"

Luis fumbled in a front pocket of his jeans, then withdrew a plastic cigarette lighter and thumbed it into life. On the rear seat of the SUV, a mass of blankets stirred and a trembling hand reached out.

"Luis, are we there now?" The voice came faint, weaker than Luis had remembered earlier in the evening.

"Not yet, Hector. I had to make a stop first. Something for myself."

The lighter sputtered and died.

"I saw someone standing beside you in the light before it went out." The words came soft with labored breathing in between. "Who did you bring?"

"He's a priest."

"I didn't ask for a priest."

"It wasn't my choice, Hector, he insisted on seeing you."

"What does he want with me?"

"I think he wants to confess you, or maybe give you Last Rites."

"Just get me to my boss, Luis, so his doctor can take care of my injuries. Do this for me. You'll be rewarded and I won't die before my time."

"Listen to me, my son," interrupted the priest. "Sooner or later, we all die. It would be best if you confess your sins and receive absolution while you still have a chance at redemption."

Luis leaned into the SUV.

"Maybe you should talk to the padre, Hector. He is a stubborn man, and the sooner your business is finished with him, then the sooner we can get on the road to your boss and the doctor. I'll just walk over there a short ways to give you two some privacy."

For ten minutes, Luis stood apart in the darkness. He heard the insistent tone of the priest gradually change to a more comforting one and then a prayer. Eventually, the priest closed the rear door and stepped back from the SUV.

Luis moved forward.

"Are you finished, padre?"

"I've done as much as I can do."

"Did he clear his conscience?"

"I believe he did, but his body is failing and his voice is almost gone. I don't believe he much time left on this earth even if you get him to a doctor."

"That's kind of what I thought too, padre."

"What will you do now, my son?"

Luis took the SUV keys out of his front jeans pocket and started for the driver's side.

"Hector gave me directions earlier on how to get to the villa of his *jefe*, so now I'll take him while he still has a little breath in him."

Luis opened the driver's door.

"Wait," cried the priest, "I thought you wanted

absolution for yourself."

"I did," replied Luis, "but that now appears to be a small matter in the scheme of things and I no longer have time if I am to take care of my business tonight. The way I see it, if God can forgive Hector for his grave sins, then I'm sure mine will be of little consequence."

He closed the door, started the engine and put it in gear.

The priest tried to open the passenger door, but it was locked. He banged on the window as the vehicle pulled away from the curb.

At the first intersection, Luis cast his voice back to the rear of the SUV.

"Hector, can you still hear me?"

Luis took the muted grunt from the rear seat as an affirmative.

"Good, because there are some things you need to know before you die. That was the last of my family you murdered tonight. I'm only taking you up on your offer of money and a job so I can get inside your boss' villa, then I'm going to kill him and as many of his men as I can. Know that I could only do this because of your help."

A frantic gurgling noise came from the back seat.

Leaning forward as he drove out of the city, Luis removed the automatic weapon and an ancient shotgun from beneath a red blanket on the front floorboards of the SUV and started arranging the weapons closer at hand.

"I tell you one more thing, Hector. Any words of comfort you might've received from that priest will mean nothing in a few minutes, because I'm taking you straight into Hell. There will be no absolution in this world for you."

ABOUT THE AUTHOR

R.T. Lawton is a retired federal law enforcement agent and a past member of the Board of Directors for the Mystery Writers of America. He has over 140 short stories in various publications, to include *Alfred Hitchcock Mystery Magazine*, the *Who Died in Here?* anthology, the *West Coast Crime Wave* e-anthology, *The Mystery Box* (an MWA anthology), the *Die Behind the Wheel* anthology, *Easyriders Magazine*, *Outlaw Biker Magazine* and ten mini-mysteries in *Woman's World Magazine*.

Connect with me online at
http://rtlawton.weebly.com

Discover other exciting eBook short stories by R.T. Lawton available now at Amazon Kindle Books and soon in paperback.

Title 1: **9** Deadly Tales

Title 2: **9** Historical Mysteries

Title 3: **9** Holiday Burglars

Title 4: **9** Twin Brothers Bail Bond Mysteries

Title 5: **31** Mini-Mysteries

BIBLIOGRAPHY

"Thieving the Ride"
Copyright © 2005 R.T. Lawton

"Not That One"
Copyright © 2004 R.T. Lawton

"To Catch a Spy"
Copyright © 2004 R.T. Lawton

"On The Perfume River"
Copyright © 2004 R.T. Lawton

"Coal Black Heart"
Copyright © 2004 R.T. Lawton

"Dearly Departed"
Copyright © 2007 R.T. Lawton

"Snitch"
Copyright © 2007 R.T. Lawton

"Shepherd of the Valley"
Copyright © 2009 R.T. Lawton

"Absolution"
Copyright © 2011 R.T. Lawton

9 HISTORICAL MYSTERIES

Armenian series
(5 stories)

During the 1850's, The Armenian, a trader of Turkic goods from the south, and his servant have come into the Cossack villages along the Terek River to hopefully conduct a profitable business with the Cossacks on the north bank and also with their enemies, the Chechens to the south in what's known as the Wild Country. In this violent land of many ethnic peoples, The Armenian tries to remain neutral to all, yet this same neutrality is what gets him drawn into solving many crimes or else acting as intermediary between warring groups. He is not a violent man, but sometimes to stay alive, he may make subtle arrangements for others to have justice fall upon them. There are many unmarked graves in the Wild Country.

1660's Paris Underworld series
(4 stories)

During the reign of France's Sun King, a young orphan boy has graduated or has graduated from, or maybe been kicked out of, Mother Margoux's Pickpocketing School for Orphans. The boy thinks he is good at his new trade, but is in fact incompetent. He lives in a criminal enclave in the ruins of an old Roman villa high up on a butte outside the walls of Paris. Every day, he must somehow earn his daily bread in order to eat, whether it is stealing in the city markets, getting lost in the catacombs below the city or working a crowd at a public hanging. And always, the older criminals find a way to get him involved in their own schemes.

TEASER

THE LITTLE NOGAI BOY

By

R.T. Lawton

In my first seven years of life I had never been robbed, but then I owned little of any value to anyone else, only the clothes on my back and a small bladed knife in the belt at my waist. My master was a different matter. He was a trader of goods and had many objects of much worth to sell on both sides of the Terek River, that winding border between the Cossack lands to the north and the Chechen tribes below.

Thus it was, those many years ago, while approaching through a shallow valley between two rolling grass hills in the Wild Country south of the river that we met the horseman. He appeared to have been waiting just for us.

#

I am Timur of the nomadic Nogai people. It is said that my long ago ancestor was of direct descent from the Great Khan, the one the Round Eyes called Temujin, the one who led our Mongols in their conquest of the known earth. His swift ponies carried the yak-tail standard north as far as the frozen lands where nights are long, and south to the deep blue waters of the Mediterranean and the sweltering jungles of the once great Hindu Kingdom. Our people raided east to the Tien Shan Mountains of China, then turned and pursued the setting sun to white-faced races beyond the edge of the Western Steppes.

At the death of Temujin rose arguments, red power struggles and old grievances. In time, our people split into the Greater Horde and the Nogai Horde and we continued our wandering ways. But in those days of my childhood, our once vast herds of horses were plundered by both Mountain and Lowland Chechen tribes, plus the bearded Cossacks who slipped south of the Terek River to raid the Wild Country. For me to survive in this decline of our once mighty people, I tied myself to the merchant who became known in this land only as The Armenian, and even I have no knowledge of his real name.

I first saw this Armenian when he came south from the Terek with a string of ponies bearing trade goods to barter in one of the distant Chechen villages. As our paths crossed, he rode wide of our yurts and horse herds travelling west in search of better grazing. In passing, we stared at each other. To me, he seemed uncomfortable on horseback and scarcely adequate to lead such a string of pack animals. His laden packs rode unbalanced and loose. He had evidently allowed his ponies to suck much air into their bellies when he tightened the leather girth to the loads on their backs. At the first sign of serious trouble, he would no doubt lose his entire stock of trade goods, and perhaps his life. I was surprised he had made it this far along from the Turkic lands where he first started. To travel this great distance, he must have been one to whom the gods had granted much luck, a circumstance we Nogai hold in high esteem.

That night, I crept away from my uncle's over-crowded yurt and followed the trail of the Armenian. No one in my uncle's family would miss this one small boy not of direct line blood. I was merely another mouth to feed, just another little boy in quilted pants and jacket with a fur cap on his head, almost indistinguishable from the other round-faced boys except my clothes were more worn and faded.

After a few hours walk, I came to the Armenian's camp on the high bank of a small creek. Here, his ponies, tied to stakes in the ground, had quickly eaten all the available grass in individual circles for as far as their short ropes would allow them. I quietly approached his riding horse, gave it several tufts of long grass I'd pulled and let the cautious beast smell the back of my hand. The smooth grey hide of his neck shivered at my first touch, his long mane rippling in the moonlight. Soon, I breathed into his damp, quivering nostrils so that he would always know me. Then I untied his rope from the wooden stake in the ground, fashioned the twisted hemp to make a halter and climbed up on the horse's back. As he slowly munched his way through the Steppes grass which he could now freely reach, I fell asleep on his back. I was at home.

Before the sun rose, I set about to make myself useful, but the sounds of my labors must have awakened the Armenian. He came out of his tent with a start, a stout piece of firewood in his hand.

"Who are you?" he demanded.

I picked up the samovar near the camp fire and poured a small cup full of fragrant dark tea. Dregs of loose black leaves swirled against the white porcelain, finally settling to the bottom. I placed the steaming cup before him and stepped back.

"I am called Timur. In the Turkic lands, it means..."

He finished my sentence, "...iron."

I nodded. Only later would I learn that he spoke many languages, a necessary trait if one is to be a successful trader of goods in this land of different tribes from many races.

Seeming to relax now that he found himself confronted only by a small, insignificant boy, the Armenian sat cross-legged on his Persian carpet in front of the tent door. This was a carpet which I had unrolled from one of his packs while the eastern sky was barely showing a pink band of light upon the distant horizon. And, I had spread this rug there upon the earth so he could avoid contact with the early morning dew upon the ground. He ignored this obvious service of comfort I had provided for him and merely sipped from his tea cup before inquiring.

"What are you doing here?"

"I am taking care of you."

His lips sputtered tea back into the cup. Dark drops fell onto the expensive Persian weave.

I would have patted him strongly on the back to ease his discomfort of swallowing hot liquid down the wrong part of his throat, but as he had not yet come to realize my true worth to him, I ignored the sudden coughing and went to gather our horses. Words from me would mean nothing; he would have to learn for himself.

By the time I returned with the animals, he had eaten

the breakfast of dried fruits and flat bread I'd laid out on a yellow napkin in one corner of the carpet. He saved no food for me, but I had already served myself from his food stocks before he awoke, so felt no hunger. I had learned early how to take care of myself in this ever changing world where life was fragile if you didn't pay attention to events around you.

For the next two days we traveled together, with him trying to do matters in the way he always had, and me rebalancing the packs before he loaded them onto our animals. Eventually, he came to accept that mine was the better way. Under my care, the pack ponies became stronger and we covered more *versts* in a day. In time, the Armenian grudgingly acknowledged my tending to his own daily needs much as a man servant would do for him.

I quickly saw he was ignorant of our ways, and could not read the thoughts of our people in the same manner he presumed to read the thoughts of other races by observing their facial expressions. At times when I caught him studying my stolid face, I realized this man truly had no idea how independent I was, nor how close I held my heritage.

In return for my labors, he protested that he would only feed me and provide a place to sleep. After all, as he frequently said, he hadn't asked me to come along.

How little he knew. If need be, I could live off this land abundant with wild game, and as for a place to sleep, I often made my bed on the back of a horse much the same as my warrior ancestors had during times of constant warfare. Truth be told, I went with him to absorb some of the luck the gods were obviously granting to this wandering Armenian, but only I was aware of my reasons.

And, that was the way things stood between us when we rode into the shallow valley between two rolling grass hills deep in the Wild Country.

As I squinted into the sun, a black silhouette at the head of the valley caught my eye. I shielded my vision with a hand to my forehead. The silhouette appeared to be a horseman waiting patiently for us to approach. How long he had been biding his time I had no way of knowing, but we were the only ones in this valley. We had to be the focus of his interest.

"Master," I pointed at the rider, "there is one who concerns me."

The Armenian gazed in the direction I had indicated. Then he settled himself in the saddle and straightened his back. "Surely a Chechen," he said at last, "one of the lowland people I hope to trade with."

Normally, I would hold my tongue, keeping my thoughts to myself, a lesson learned at the rough hands of my uncle who believed only men had words worth listening to, not the small mouths of little boys. But, there was something in this Chechen's manner, like a lean wolf waiting patiently to feed, knowing full well that his meal was coming to him. I glanced round at the hill crests on either side of the valley. No other riders appeared in view.

"This may be one of those Abreks," I tried to explain, "a brigand from the mountains."

"Then I'll trade with him," replied the Armenian. "His coins are as good as any."

"Do you at least have a weapon to defend us if necessary?" I inquired.

"I do," he said, but seemed unconcerned. "There should be a flintlock pistol in amongst the bundle of Turkic trade knives in a pack on one of the ponies behind us. I have never seen need to carry a weapon upon my person." He turned to look me in the eyes. "Take heed, little one, physical violence only breeds more violence. It is better to use one's brain."

I tried to keep my face impassive, only groaning silently to myself at this turn of bad luck. I had obviously made an error in judgment and therefore tied my future to an idiot. If we both survived this trip south, then my master was truly more blessed by the gods than even I had hoped.

As we continued up the trail over rising ground to the head of the valley, the sun rose higher and I could see the rider more clearly. His boots were made of soft Morocco leather, and above them he wore blue, loose-fitting trousers that tied below the knees with leather straps. Beneath his open sheepskin vest, he wore his *beshmet*, a tight-waisted almost knee-length shirt with long sleeves. A wide leather belt encircled his waist, and here was thrust a long dagger of good Turkic quality. His dark face showed a trace of Tartar blood with a short cropped beard dyed red while his head was clean-shaven in the fashion of many young Chechen braves.

His welcome sounded genuine, but I suspected otherwise.

"Good day to you, travelers upon my land."

We halted some distance below him and were forced

to look upward at his position of dominance. I couldn't help noticing the flintlock musket, inset with bright Turkic silver, which rested across his lap. As yet it wasn't pointed in our direction, but still I had a feeling.

"I thought this land belonged to all Chechens," ventured the Armenian.

"Wherever Yarbay goes," replied the rider as he touched the flat of his palm to his chest, "that land where I stand belongs only to me, and all who pass through must pay me *yassak*."

He gestured toward us, and even though this Chechen spoke his words with a friendly smile on his face, I knew he hungered for our trade goods.

"Abrek," I whispered to my master.

"A matter of tribute," said the Armenian aloud as if he hadn't heard me. "I see." He nodded his head as though he'd come to a decision known only to himself. "Then we will ride around your piece of land and find others to trade with." He reined his horse to the right.

I kept my pony where he stood.

The Chechen stepped his horse sideways to block my master's new path. The musket had now come off of Yarbay's lap, the butt of the flintlock resting on his thigh with the barrel pointing up at the bright blue of sky overhead..........

To read the rest of the story and eight more, get 9 Historical Mysteries by R.T. Lawton

Made in the USA
Lexington, KY
13 September 2019